A RESPECTABLE HOUSE

Seven years ago, Kitty made the biggest mistake of her life when she was tricked into eloping with a scoundrel. Now her husband is dead at the hands of London's most dangerous criminal — and he's after Kitty, too. Guarding Kitty and her six-year-old daughter Ann is dark, cynical Nicholas Dacre, who presents a reckless face to the world, frustrated by the constraints of his family name. He is as scarred as Kitty, but in her company, the rigid tenets he grew up with are tumbling faster than the autumn leaves . . .

JAN JONES

A RESPECTABLE HOUSE
A Newmarket Regency

Complete and Unabridged

LINFORD
Leicester

First published in Great Britain in 2018

First Linford Edition
published 2020

Copyright © 2018 by Jan Jones
All rights reserved

*A catalogue record for this book is available
from the British Library.*

ISBN 978–1–4448–4519–8

Published by
Ulverscroft Limited
Anstey, Leicestershire

Set by Words & Graphics Ltd.
Anstey, Leicestershire
Printed and bound in Great Britain by
T. J. International Ltd., Padstow, Cornwall

A Respectable House

is dedicated to all the survivors

People who have been through so much and come out the other side

Dramatis Personae

in order of appearance (mostly)

Kitty Eastwick (aka Catherine Redding) — a lady on the run
[Previously in *A Rational Proposal*]

Ann — Kitty's daughter
[Previously in *A Rational Proposal*]

Verity Bowman — Kitty's half-sister
[Previously in *A Rational Proposal*]

Charles Congreve —Verity's betrothed, attorney, member of the Pool
[Previously in *The Kydd Inheritance*, *An Unconventional Act*, *A Rational Proposal*]

Nicholas Dacre — enigmatic rake, member of the Pool
[Previously in *A Rational Proposal*]

Adam Prettyman — landowner and former actor, member of the Pool [Previously in *Fair Deception*, *An Unconventional Act*, *A Rational Proposal*]

Viscount Perivale — an irritating nobleman

The Duke of Rutland — a very noble noble

Lord Alexander Rothwell — politician, member of the Pool [Previously in *Fortunate Wager*]

John Bowman — Kitty's full brother

Chesterfield and Richards — Perivale's cronies

Molly Turner — Kitty's friend, seamstress and lady of the night [Previously in *A Rational Proposal*]

Ma Turner — Molly's mother, laundress

Jenny Prettyman — Adam's wife [Previously in *An Unconventional Act, A Rational Proposal*]

Mrs Hennessy — A very expensive lady indeed

Mr & Mrs Green — the gardener and his wife

Fred Grimes — hackney driver

Selina Bowman — John's wife

Various servants, grooms, townsmen, race-goers and children

Other characters in the *Furze House Irregulars* series:

Benedict Fitzgilbert — head of the Pool

Lilith Fitzgilbert — his sister

Julia Congreve — Charles's sister

Oh, and

Flint — don't ask. Really, don't ask

Author's Note

A Respectable House is the second of the Furze House Irregulars books and begins immediately after the events in *A Rational Proposal*. You do not have to have read *A Rational Proposal* to enjoy this story, though naturally I'd be delighted if you read that one too!

A Rational Proposal introduced Verity Bowman and Charles Congreve. In *A Respectable House*, it is the turn of Verity's half-sister Kitty Eastwick and Charles's friend Nicholas Dacre to take the stage.

The third and fourth books in the series are *A Scholarly Application*, featuring Verity's friend Lilith Fitzgilbert, and *A Practical Arrangement*, which is Charles's sister Julia Congreve's story.

1

Dead. Simon was dead; knifed outside a gaming hell on his way to Bow Street to answer a charge of fraud.

Kitty Eastwick felt too dazed to move. She sat in the elegant drawing room in Grosvenor Street where she and her six-year-old daughter had taken refuge this morning, hardly able to believe it. She had screwed up her courage so hard to escape with Ann and be free of Simon's schemes. It seemed impossible that he was no longer filling her horizon with uncertainty and fear.

It was over an hour now since her half-sister Verity had erupted into the room with the news of Simon's arrest and murder. Even under normal conditions, Kitty would have needed a period of sustained reflection to consider how

1

best to go on. Verity, however, was a stranger to sustained reflection. After the tumult of disclosures and discoveries that had followed that first shocking statement, Kitty was only just starting to take in her wholly unlooked-for liberty. The roaring gale of relief blowing through her mind was tempered by new, bitter knowledge. Her husband's murder wasn't the only revelation that had come to light during this past hour.

Papa had *paid* Simon to elope with her. Even at the beginning, the charismatic man she had promised to obey and who had made her life a lattice of insecurity, hadn't been in love with her. Kitty had been a commodity to both her father and her husband. All the shame, the pain, the humiliation. The hard-fought acceptance of blame because running away with Simon was her own mistake to start with. The obstinate determination over seven long years to make what she could of this life because she had brought it upon herself . . . it had all been based on a falsehood. She was a thousand times a fool.

Verity shook her arm. That was another astonishing thing: even though they'd been parted all this time, her family was nevertheless wrapping her in warmth, enveloping her and Ann in care. 'Kitty, are you listening?' repeated Verity. 'You have to get away. We think your husband was killed to prevent him betraying the evil man he worked for. Flint may think *you* know his real identity as well. That means you are in danger.'

Kitty stirred. Ever since reaching Grosvenor Street, she'd been desperate to travel on, clear of London and out of Simon's reach. Now, just as she was secure, they were saying his shadowy employer, Flint, whom a quarter of London feared with good reason, might be after her. It was a further impossibility piled upon the rest. The human heart cannot take that much agitation.

'Kitty! You must get Ann to safety.'

Ann. The daughter she would walk

through fire for. The short sentence broke through Kitty's paralysis. 'Yes,' she said. 'Yes, of course I must, but I *don't* know who Flint is. He is a code-word, a lurking menace, not to be spoken of. Simon has never told me his real name. He never shares information.' She corrected herself, feeling a frightening reminder of Flint's reach. 'Shared. Simon never shared information. What he had, he held close, whether it was possessions like me and Ann, or knowledge that he might use for gain. He'd never water down secrets by telling anyone else about them.'

Verity shook her head. 'Flint cannot be sure of that. And even if he *did* know, he holds life very cheaply. This is the man who burnt down an accommodation house as a warning, with all the women still inside. They escaped, but there was no guarantee they would. He might kill you and Ann simply to snip off the end of a thread that could lead to him. You must get out of London and away to Furze House tonight, and I

4

must not come with you as I dearly wish, but instead shall make a great fuss here about where you might be to throw any observers off the scent. And Kitty, you must not use the name Eastwick. It is sufficiently uncommon that any enquiry in Newmarket will find you straight away.'

'That was the only honourable thing Simon ever gave me. So be it. I won't return to being Catherine Bowman though. My father sold me into marriage. I will never use his name again.'

'You can think of another on the journey. Invent yourself a second marriage. Quickly, collect what you and Ann need. Charles's friend Nicholas Dacre who helped you this morning is to fetch you from the livery stables. I will send further word on Monday with Adam Prettyman. Do you remember the Chartwell Players or had you left Newmarket before they changed cir-cuit? Adam was the actor manager, but is now married to Jenny Rooke and is the estate manager at Rooke Hall. He has been staying with Charles. You will know him, for he is large and fair and has the kindest eyes ever. Oh, do hurry, Kitty. Go with Mama to pack for tonight. Adam will bring the rest on Monday.'

★   ★   ★

So here Kitty was, her mind still numb but starting to work again, speeding through the night in a gentleman's fast-travelling coach with Ann asleep in one corner and the gentleman himself — an unknown quality — regarding her from the shadows of the opposite seat. This morning she had simply been grateful for his efficiency, so anxious had she been to get herself and Ann out of Henrietta Street and into the waiting hackney cab without attracting attention. Now she must make more of an effort.

'I must thank you,' she said, her voice sounding strange to her own ears. 'This is twice today you have rescued us.'

Nicholas Dacre moved an elegant shoulder dismissively. 'Think nothing of it. I had always intended on travelling to the final Newmarket meeting of the year.'

'But not at night,' said Kitty, 'with your bag packed in a scramble, no valet to attend you and no dinner inside you.'

A sardonic smile drifted across her companion's face. 'Firstly, my valet never comes to race meetings. It does not suit his dignity. Second, the day he does not pack me an adequate bag for any eventuality is the day he would throw himself off the nearest bridge into the Thames. Third, I frequently miss dinner.'

Kitty blinked, distracted. 'Why?'

'Largely because it annoys my family. We can bespeak something when we change horses if you are hungry.'

'There is food packed in the basket. For myself, I do not believe I will ever be hungry again. Ann might be when she wakes.' Kitty glanced at her

7

daughter, fierce protectiveness welling up inside her as it had since the moment Ann had been born. At times, Ann had been all that kept her going. 'You have no need to be concerned about us, Mr Dacre. Verity and Charles were insistent you behave exactly as normal, for fear of stirring up questions. Did you know they are engaged?'

'So Charles said. I foretold it several days ago.' He stretched, and now Kitty realised there was a sense of contained power inside his well-fitting coat. 'As for me, I make a point of being unpredictable. Anything that infuriates the Dacre household is never wasted.'

Spoilt, she concluded, but then, weren't all men? She no longer had any veneration for the opposite sex. Life with Simon had exposed her to more vice than she had ever imagined existed. However, Verity's Charles was a good man and this friend of his was putting himself out in order to hurry her and Ann away from London, so she kept her tongue behind her teeth. She was well practised at that. 'As you please. I will remain in the carriage with Ann. I apologise if I appear distracted. This morning all I was aware of was that your friends would try to take my husband in charge for fraud. Since then we have discovered — through a memorandum he deliberately concealed inside my cookery book — that seven years ago Simon was acting as Flint's agent in order to blackmail my father and he was also paid to elope with me.' She could not help sounding bitter.

His voice softened. 'Charles told me, yes. My sympathies. It is always a shock, to find oneself the object of deception.'

'Thank you. In truth I do not know why it should hurt so much when he has done so many worse things since.'

'Logic has little effect on the emotions, in my experience.'

'I believe you are right. It also seems unfair that I cannot even dwell properly on his infamy because I have such an overriding fear of being discovered by

Flint. Please understand that I am not disparaging you in this. I know your horses are fast and Furze House is an unknown address to him — I also know he has a long reach. I do not doubt my sister's ability to make it seem as if I am still in town, but I cannot make the mistake of complacency. From the whispers, the side-murmuring, the disappearances and significant silences that abound every day in our streets, Flint would no sooner take an apparently blind alley at face value than he would fly.'

Nicholas Dacre's casual air vanished. The sense of leashed power from him redoubled. He sat forward, taking Kitty's hands and looking at her intently. 'We call Flint the shadow master between ourselves. Do you know more of him than you have said?'

Walk forward . . .

Kitty jerked at the sudden memory. She freed her hands so her companion would not feel them tremble. 'I have impressions,' she said, 'as everyone does. Shadow master is a good description. Flint has an unseen presence. There is a lot of fear. Simon collected money for him, but I never saw any of it. I don't know how it was passed on. He was not his only bagman, so someone will take over his collections, but for you to watch all the brothels and hells in London to find a path back to him would be to invite disaster on the watcher. Flint . . . ' She swallowed. 'Flint likes to punish.'

Mr Dacre nodded thoughtfully and sat back against the squabs. 'I keep a change of horses at Hatfield. We won't stop until then. I recommend you join your daughter in sleep. You will find a rug under the seat.'

Kitty said nothing at the abrupt dismissal. Once she would have bridled. Now, she was thankful to be left alone. She tucked the rug around Ann, spreading what was left across her own lap, then leaned back, staring into the darkness, trying to forget.

Walk forward . . .

She felt herself tremble again. Nicholas Dacre's question had unlocked a closet she had slammed shut four years ago. She hadn't precisely lied about not knowing more. After all, she hadn't seen the whispering man's face, nor did she know for sure that it had been Flint. Perhaps she should say something anyway.

Walk forward . . .

Despite her rigid control, she remembered the black cotton hood and the cold impassive whisper. It still had the power to make her sick with dread. Kitty half-closed her eyes, willing the fear back into its closet. No, she couldn't speak of it, not to a man she didn't know, no matter how well recommended he was.

She focused her gaze on Nicholas Dacre. He was worth looking at. Seven years ago his combination of dark good looks, loose-limbed grace and easy assumption of rank would have been irresistible to rebellious, wayward Kitty Bowman. That girl was long gone. She occasionally traced the ghost of her in a shop window or in the joy of a trill of music from a piano workshop, but mostly she existed only in memory. Seven years had replaced her confident overtures with defences, had caged her in wariness, had stilled her tongue until every word was thought out before being uttered. 'I need a new name,' she remembered.

He nodded. 'I'll think of one.'

And against all the odds, Kitty slept.

★ ★ ★

Beautiful, thought Nick, contemplating the fine bone structure and soft dark hair of the sleeping woman as his new chestnut team sped the carriage through the night towards Newmarket. He'd thought so this morning when he'd collected her and the child from her rooms and delivered them to Grosvenor Street. That was supposed to have been the end of his involvement: an anonymous courier, seen once in the neighbourhood and then gone, with nothing to connect him to her disappearance. But that was before the husband she was escaping from had been knifed in the street and they'd realised she too was likely to be in danger. Nick, with his fast horses and mercurial lifestyle, was the best person to get her to safety.

He looked at her again, her face a pale oval in the hurrying shadows. He knew only the bare bones of her history. She and her older brother had been the children of the late Mr Bowman's first wife, who had been barely cold in her coffin before he'd remarried. It must have been a lonely time for a child. He could identify with that.

Had she always been so still and quiet, playing down her beauty? Sleep smoothed the care lines in her face. There was no hint now of the wariness that characterised her every move. Awake, she was too thin, too watchful, wound tight inside. No young woman should have need of such vigilance. If Simon Eastwick hadn't already been murdered, Nick might have volunteered for his despatch.

He glanced out of the window, alert

to possible danger, but there was nothing out of the usual. He wondered what the rest of the Pool — the loose 'pool of talent' Benedict Fitzgilbert had gathered to covertly combat London's crime — were doing back in the capital. It couldn't help but irk Nick that he'd been relegated to the role of bodyguard while the rest of them closed in on the elusive shadow master, but that was one reason the Pool was successful. Each of them had their own talents. Charles's was the law, Fitz provided finance and position, Alex Rothwell brought politics and the radical movement to the mix, Nick himself added the devil-may-care trappings and moral flexibility of the rake. Only he knew how much of that was a mask.

Once the potential hazards of Hampstead Heath were behind them he dozed lightly, aware of other travellers passing, satisfied that his coachman and groom were watching the road with a care for his horses. The journey would have been safer in that respect by daylight, but it was full moon and his men were experienced.

The child shifted. Mrs Eastwick's hand moved to reassure her, though both were asleep. Nick knew little of children but the girl seemed biddable enough, with the same grey eyes and elfin good looks as her mother. Six years old, Charles had said. Nick could see why Mrs Eastwick wanted to get her away from the streets.

Neither of them stirred further until the carriage was running into Hatfield.

'Be easy,' said Nick, seeing his passenger's eyes open and her body tense for danger. 'We are making good time and have had no trouble.'

'Trouble?' There was an edge of alarm to her voice.

'Over Finchley Common and Hampstead Heath. I didn't expect any as it's a moonlit night and any watcher can see this is a gentleman's fast coach, not a family carriage, but it's as well to be prepared.'

She sat up. 'My stepmother's former

betrothed was killed by highwaymen twenty years ago. That was why Flint was blackmailing Papa. Papa ordered it, you see, to remove the obstacle so he could marry her instead. We didn't know until today. It is still today, isn't it?'

He smiled faintly. 'It is around nine of the evening. We should make Newmarket by midnight. I keep a fresh team at the inn here and they'll harness us another team again at the Red Lion at Whittlesford.'

'That sounds . . . expensive.' There was neither approval nor censure in her tone, but he remembered her carefully-mended gloves as he'd handed her into the carriage earlier and heat rose in his cheeks.

'I travel this route frequently,' he said brusquely. 'My grandfather is a twisted, scheming devil, but the one thing he and I are agreed on is the necessity for good cattle. He considers it my only redeeming feature. Whatever else he may cut from my allowance, stabling for my horses will never suffer.'

'An allowance.'

Strange how even the most noncommittal words could stab. 'Yes. An allowance. For acting as his messenger boy. For dancing attendance on him. For continuing to live in his house in order to feed his ego. If you ever run out of nightmares, I will tell you about my family.'

She gave a short laugh. 'I believe you are safe from that eventuality.'

The coach slowed and made the turn into the inn yard. Nick pulled the window blinds down, ashamed at his loss of control. Beneath them, the springs dealt with the change of surface. He listened to his groom greeting the ostlers and the familiar sounds of his horses being unhitched, but he made no move to get out of the carriage.

'I have given orders that I am not to be disturbed,' he said. 'It will no doubt be a disappointment to the landlord, but there are sufficient other travellers on the road to ply with overpriced refreshment that he is unlikely to feel the loss of our custom. By the by, I have thought of a name for you. How do you like Mrs Redding? A respectable widow with a small jointure, very happy to be acting as housekeeper for her sister on the one hand and also for a philanthropic foundation that lets out rooms to women of good character.'

'Respectable?' she said with wry amusement. 'I had best cudgel my memory and remember the way of it. Thank you. You are going to a great deal of trouble for me.'

'You are the sister of my friend's intended wife. If that were not reason alone, my associates and I object very strongly to the creeping tide of vice in London. We aim to curb it. Keeping you safe is part of that. Incidentally, we will also be staying at Furze House from time to time. It will make a useful meeting place for the Pool, as we call ourselves, out of the public eye.'

She raised her eyebrows. 'Staying at

Furze House? You do not *look* like a woman of good character.'

He laughed, surprised and charmed by her wit. 'There appeared from the outside to be a separate wing we can utilise. I reconnoitred it the last time I was here after Charles told me Verity had her heart set on the place. Do you remember the house at all?'

She shook her head. 'It is seven years since I left Newmarket. I have endeavoured to forget everything. Life takes enough handling without the added distraction of hankering for the past.' She turned her head. 'What's that?' she said sharply.

Nick listened. There was a swell of noise in the inn yard. Horses' hooves clattering. Raised voices, slurred with ale and brandy.

One voice was clearer than the rest. 'Look at that! Isn't that Dacre's coach and the chestnut team he was bragging about? Damned if I don't challenge him to a race. What do you say?'

As the sound of boisterous approval

came nearer, Nick swore and reached for the door handle. 'Curse it, they mustn't see you. Drunk tongues are loose tongues. I'll deflect them.'

'There is no time.' Before Nick's appalled and dumbfounded eyes his companion swiftly flipped the rug so it concealed her daughter, then swung her legs up along the seat and raised her skirts. 'I'm afraid you must sacrifice your reputation, Mr. Dacre. If you could shield my face, please? There is no knowing whether your friends have played cards with my husband at some time. I could easily have served them ale or wine. Hurry, please.'

Lord, but she was game. Nick took less than a second to boggle at her courage as she tugged off her shawl and loosened her bodice, before he was hurriedly adjusting the fall of his breeches and angling himself to cover her. He heard the scrape of boots on cobbles and the rattle of the door handle, then he grunted suggestively as a cold rush of air entered and Viscount Perivale's voice slurred, 'Ho there, Dacre, no hiding away. Fifty guineas says you can't get to the Green Man before us.'

Underneath him, the newly-christened Mrs Redding gave a husky moan of pleasure, bringing a startled quickening to his body.

'Out of luck, Perry,' he growled, the gruffness not altogether feigned. 'Bother someone else. I'm in no mood to hurry. And shut the door. You're letting in a draught.'

There was a stunned silence, then loud guffaws, a slap on his rump and the door was closed. The sounds of merriment retreated, followed by shouts to grooms and horses.

'That'll get back to my grandfather within the week,' said Nick into the silence. Her hair tickled his nose and he raised his head. 'Something new to scandalise him with. Save me having to think of anything else to keep the villain on his toes. Society might cut me for a while, mind.' He was talking at random and he knew it.

Outside, the horses' bits clinked softly as the chestnuts were led away and the new team hitched up. The carriage began to move forward. His companion cleared her throat as if they were conversing at a soiree. 'If you could perhaps move, Mr Dacre?'

'I'm not sure I can.' Nick spoke nothing but the truth. She was warm and vital and disturbing beneath him. He could feel the rapid staccato of her heart beating against his waistcoat. Controlled and guarded she may be in the normal course of events, but for a few impossible, incredible seconds just then, she hadn't radiated respectability at all. He was attempting to come to terms with it.

'If you are concerned about embarrassing me,' she said dryly, 'I rather think we have passed that point. I see I needn't have worried about your reputation.'

The dry tone had its effect. He regained mastery over his limbs and pushed himself off and on to the opposite seat, his face flaming. She sat and composedly rearranged bodice and shawl as if what they had just feigned had been nothing.

'Your daughter,' managed Nick, fastening his buttons with fingers that almost refused to work. 'Is she all right?'

The blanket was folded back to reveal the child deep in slumber. 'She has learnt to sleep through disturbances. Are we likely to meet more of your friends at the next change?'

'They are not my friends.' Aware that he sounded churlish, he added, 'There was nothing in it. Perivale bets on anything that isn't nailed down. Come the last post, he'll be up there at the pearly gates running a book on the number of feathers in the Archangel's wings. To answer your question, I do not believe many people change horses at the Red Lion, but to forestall anything of the sort happening again, I shall alight and lean against the carriage door.' He took a deep breath, unsettled for a number of reasons; the most acceptable one being that she, not he, had thought of the ruse so fast. He was also disconcerted that she had put aside the brief intimate contact so easily. 'That was quick thinking. Forgive me, I should apologise for my very natural reaction, but I find myself unable to.'

She had a small dismissive smile for that, one that said he was a man and thus it was to be expected. 'I believe we might forget the incident now.'

Forget that? Forget the feeling of her body under his? Forget the swirl of instant, compelling heat? She asked the impossible. 'You are an unusual woman, Mrs . . . Mrs Redding.'

'If your shadow master finds me, I am dead,' she said flatly. 'If I am fortunate, he will not use me for his own pleasure first. My care is all for Ann. There is no mortification I would not endure for her sake. I would kill Flint and face the hangman's noose rather than let him lay one finger on her. You and your friends are searching for him. You know what a vile monster he is.'

'Yes,' said Nick. *Mortification. Oh good.*

'Then you understand there is nothing I would not baulk at to keep my daughter safe.'

Baulk. Splendid.

A glimmer of a smile crossed her face. She rested her hand briefly on his. 'I chose my words ill. I apologise. It was not so very mortifying. Thank you for your restraint.'

2

Had she offended him? It was difficult to tell behind that cynical mask. Probably. Men were apt to think themselves irresistible. It would have hurt his pride that she hadn't lingered underneath him, even in masquerade. He was, however, gentleman enough not to proceed. Was that why she'd suggested it? Because she'd known she would be safe? No, she'd done it instinctively for Ann and her own skin. But a whispered voice in her head said that if Nicholas Dacre had turned fiction into fact, it might not have been too much of a hardship to take the consequences.

She felt her face heat in the darkness of the carriage. After everything she'd done out of necessity . . . to even be thinking such thoughts! She did not deserve to be rescued. 'May we have the blinds up?' she said aloud. 'Is it safe? I should like to see a little of where we are going.'

He stirred and released the loops. 'Certainly. We can pull them down again if another vehicle approaches. We had best work on your story for Newmarket. Who was your husband? What did he die of? Killed abroad is easiest.'

'Not the army. I am done with military men. A clerk, perhaps?'

Her companion nodded. 'A clerk in a shipping office. That is nicely anonymous. He can have had consumption.'

'The docks are sadly unhealthy places to work,' she agreed. 'I think his name must have been John. No one would expect me to invent a husband with the same name as my brother.' She pushed a stray lock of hair back from her face. 'What of my brother? I am likely to see John eventually, even though Kennet End is a little way out of Newmarket. It will surely filter back to him that I am returned. Indeed, once

28

Verity arrives there can be no conceal-
ment at all.'

'Then the story must stand up to
scrutiny, and all who know the truth
must be forewarned. Have you been in
contact with your home since you left?'

'No, not with anybody. Not until
Verity found me. I thought . . . ' She
looked away from him for a moment as
she beat back the remembered misery.
'I thought they had all of them cut me
off. We only realised a few days ago that
my father must have destroyed my
letters before they even reached Mama.'
She saw a flicker of puzzlement cross
his face. 'I beg your pardon. She is my
stepmother, but I always call her
Mama. I hardly remember my own as
she died when I was so young. It was
almost the worst thing, thinking Mama
hated me for eloping.'

He brushed her hand, not intrusively,
but for comfort. 'I am sorry. But the
estrangement means there will be
nothing to contradict our new story.
You will be remembered around the

town, I take it? And your reason for leaving? Then let it be thought Captain Eastwick deceived you, you separated and later married the illusionary John Redding. Your widowed status is not an issue, but I fear it will be remarked that you have no maid or servants to do the work of the house.'

The strangest sense of shock ran through Kitty. She gazed at him, stricken. She really was returning to her own world. 'I hadn't given that a thought. There has been no money for maids since I left. I must visit the registry office, I suppose. It will be another thing to accustom myself to. My being alone will not be a problem, for my friend Molly Turner is to join me in a week or two. Verity arranged it all. There has never been any stopping my sister once she gets a plan in her head. Molly and her mother are to open up the laundry at the back of the house. Fred Grimes the hackney driver will come with them, I think. Then there are two women Simon sold into a brothel.

Do you know about them? Verity says the younger one is very young indeed. She thinks it will suit Hannah to be a proper servant again. She has been appallingly mistreated.'

'I do know about it and was frankly amazed at the idea. Will you not mind, having those women in your house?'

Kitty could see why he might think so. 'You mean because it was my husband who seduced them before abandoning them? No, it is many years since I ceased to love him. It may be awkward at first, but we were all wronged by Simon. It makes us sisters.'

'You are remarkable. Incidentally, I must tell you I have met your friend Molly. No, not in *that* way,' he added, evidently seeing the flash of amusement in her eyes. 'I tried to find out about Flint from her over supper. I liked her. A refreshing woman. Very businesslike. You do not intend letting any of them carry on their . . . profession in Newmarket?'

Stop Molly doing what comes naturally? 'Everyone must eat,' murmured

Kitty, then relented at his startled look, surprised at how mirthful the tiny joke had made her feel. 'There is no need to be alarmed. It is Verity's hope that Furze House will support itself by more conventional means. Molly's mending and her mother's laundry, for example. It will be a respectable house.' *Or at least discreet, which amounts to nearly the same thing.*

He gave her an unconvinced look. Kitty reminded herself that he *had* after all met her friend. 'There is something else,' he said. 'I gave my word to keep you safe, but with no maid or companion, for propriety's sake I should not stay in the house.'

She laughed aloud at that. 'Housekeepers do not have companions, Mr Dacre. They *provide* the respectability, they do not require it for themselves. In any case it is difficult to further compromise the widow of a murdered man who dealt in duplicity and fraud every day of his life. Pray do not concern yourself with my reputation. I assure you it is beyond repair.'

'We are building you anew, remember?' Then he added abruptly, 'My name is Nicholas. My friends call me Nick.'

She smiled. 'And I am Catherine, or Kitty. Anything but Kit. Simon called me that. Please . . . Nicholas . . . I beg you will stay in Furze House as you planned to do. If it is as large as Verity described, I should be very glad to have another person there. I am unused to space after so long.' And, as he still looked undecided, she added, 'Also, there may be furniture to move.'

He spread his hands. 'Appealing to masculine pride is a low blow. How can I refuse?'

He was as good as his word and stretched his legs in the yard of the Red Lion while his men changed the horses, but this time the halt brought no unwelcome disturbance. Kitty listened, intrigued, as he murmured to the horses before they were led away and then greeted the new team as if they were friends.

'You are fond of your horses,' she

said, once they were on their way again.

'I confess I frequently like them better than people. Having a large stable at my disposal is the only circumstance that makes living in my grandfather's household tolerable. Those greys we used for the middle stretch are not quite as good a team as the chestnuts; these new ones are faster. Do you ride?'

'I did, before I was deceived into eloping.' She paused. 'That is not entirely accurate. I wanted to elope. I was headstrong, wayward and very restless. I made it easy for Simon to deceive me. With hindsight I was lucky my father paid him to marry me, else I'd have been sold into prostitution, like those other unfortunate girls, as soon as he was tired of me. As it was, he . . . ' She clamped her mouth shut on what she'd so nearly let out.

Nicholas looked at her quizzically.

She shook her head, dismayed at her near-lapse. 'A closed carriage is a dangerous thing. There is too much of the confessional about it. From now on I am Catherine Redding. Kitty Eastwick no longer exists.' *Would that my memories were as easily obliterated.*

They reverted to silence. Glancing at her companion, Kitty fancied his own thoughts were no more pleasant than hers. As they crossed Newmarket Heath, however, he grew alert, his bearing subtly dangerous as he scrutinised the scrubby grassland surrounding them for potential attackers.

At the top of the rise into Newmarket, he relaxed. Kitty looked out of the window and her heart gave an unexpected leap.

'What is it?' asked Nicholas.

'This,' she said, wondering at her own gladness. 'This road, with the town nestling at the bottom. I thought I had forgotten it all, but some things stay with you, it seems.'

He gave her a swift smile. 'Early memories. Before everything shattered.'

'Yes, that must be it. Do you feel the same way about your home?'

He shifted on the seat. 'Not my home, no. That has never been comfortable.

School, though. I was happy there. And Cambridge. That was where I met Charles. He was a lot more diligent than me. Though I'm the better fencer.' He leaned out of the window and called up to the coachman. 'Look out for the large houses on the left. The third or fourth, I think we want. Furze House. Just before the terrace on the other side.'

There was an answering shout from above, and within a couple of minutes they were turning between two stone pillars and rumbling to a halt. Nicholas opened the door and the smell of fresh country air immediately assailed Kitty. Another memory. He handed her out. She lurched at standing upright after so many hours and was caught to him. The air, the sense of safety, of being back home, and the feeling of his lean body against hers made her stumble again.

'Forgive me. I have been sitting for too long,' she said. She kept her hand on his arm for balance as she turned to look at Furze House. It was even larger than she had expected, its windows dark under the bright moonlight. 'How do we get in?'

Nicholas's expression was rueful and amused. 'I have no idea. Rouse the gardener?'

'I suppose so.' She looked doubtfully at the shuttered cottage at the far end of the drive, then Ann called out, a small worried cry of waking and finding herself alone in a strange place. Instantly, Kitty spun back to the coach and scooped her into her arms, all hesitancy forgotten.

They crunched their way down the gravelled drive past the house. As they approached the gardener's dwelling, Kitty saw a flicker from a candle through a small window. 'Someone has heard the carriage,' she said, relieved she wouldn't be waking them after all.

Nicholas thumped on the door.

'Who's there?' came the wavering reply.

'My name is Catherine Redding,' said Kitty through the door. 'My sister

Verity Bowman has taken this house for us, but I have come on ahead. I am sorry it is so very late, but we need the key to get in. My sister charged me to ask if the honey from my brother's hives had found favour with you?'

A bolt was pulled back, and the door opened a fraction. Two elderly people stood in silhouette, alike in nightcaps and shawls, peering hesitantly out. 'Oh, you've a child,' said the more obviously female bundle, and the atmosphere lightened.

'Yes, this is Ann. She is named for my mother, Mrs Bowman, whom I think you have met. She has only just woken after the journey, but I will bring her across tomorrow to meet you properly. I am afraid we are all of us a little sleepy at the moment.'

'The beds . . . ' began the gardener's wife.

'I have bed linen,' said Kitty. 'Truly, all we need is to get in.'

A large wrought iron key was proffered through the gap in the door, then the door was closed and the bolt drawn.

'God bless you,' said Kitty, and wondered at herself for falling so easily back into the country way of speaking.

Nicholas took the key. As he let them into Furze House, he cast a look back at the road, where coaches and curricles were still bowling down the High Street even though it was late. 'I need to get the carriage out of sight,' he said, 'then I'll send the men and the horses to the White Hart for the night. Time enough tomorrow to see if anything can be made of the stable. Do you have a tinder box? Can you get some candles lit in here?'

'Yes, I'll see to that,' said Kitty, 'you deal with the carriage.'

He hurried away. Holding Ann by the hand, Kitty looked around the shadowy hallway of her new home. The rumble of wheels outside grew fainter.

'There is a candle, Mama,' said Ann, pointing to a table at the foot of the stairs.

'So there is.' Their voices echoed amongst the sparse furnishings. She gave her basket to the child. 'Can you find me the tinder box? Then we can close this door.'

While Ann rummaged amongst the contents for the small, circular tin, Kitty moved further into the house. Not since she'd left Kennet End had she been in a hallway so spacious, at the foot of stairs so handsome. An open door to the left gave on to an airy sitting room with squares of moonlight falling across a patterned carpet and a gilt, scroll-worked sofa. It was so beautiful and so perfect it took her breath away.

'Bring the basket and candle in here, Ann,' she said. 'There is a window seat with plenty of light from outside.' And as her daughter came into the room, she gathered her into a hug. 'We are home. We are truly home.'

★   ★   ★

Nick swore and sweated with his men as they shifted the carriage past the house, past the outbuildings, through a small yard and into the coach-house. He hadn't given its distinctive burgundy-and-gilt paintwork a thought until Perry had recognised it in Hatfield and hauled open the door. But as the journey had continued and he'd seen Catherine's tension at every passing vehicle, he'd remembered just why they were fleeing London at this late hour. Now he wanted every tell-tale trace of burgundy hidden from sight. The last thing he needed was Viscount Perivale and his cronies hammering on the door of Furze House, intent on dragging him out to Crockford's to gamble the small hours away.

Once done, he sent the men and horses to the White Hart and carried the last of the baggage through the front door, which he closed and bolted behind him. Already the house seemed lived-in. The soft yellow glow of a candle lit the hall. Catherine was halfway up the stairs with a second candle in one hand, holding Ann by the other. She turned and glanced down with a smile.

'Thank you. We are going to look for bedchambers. I am leaving the back premises for tonight. If you are hungry, there is a pie in the basket and a piece of beef.'

The candlelight, the graceful staircase and the woman herself holding her young daughter by the hand took Nick's breath away. They were all the warm, loving images of home that had never been his. This, this had been missing all his life. He didn't want reminding of it. He didn't need the lack of a caring family thrust in front of him. Damn it, why had he not bespoke a room at the White Hart? His throat worked as he tried to get some words out.

'Can I help?' he managed.

Her smile became mischievous. 'If you hurry, you can choose the best room instead of letting Ann have all her own way. She is very full of herself, having found a whole box of candles under the window seat in the sitting room.'

He grinned and ascended to join them. 'Clever girl. As for my room, as long as it has a mattress it will do for tonight.'

'I am hoping we will have rather more than that. Everything has happened so fast today that I forgot to ask, but I believe Verity said the house was furnished.'

'At least in part. I know very little more. I have not been involved until now.' *Except to tease Charles by adding his voice to Fitz's in support for a base at Newmarket for the Pool.*

'And should not be now. It was good of you to bring us, whatever you say. Now I am here, sixty miles from London and with the door closed against the world, I feel very much less anxious. Do please forget anything foolish I may have said in the coach. I promise we will not interrupt your racing this week. You will hardly know we are in residence at all.'

He stared. He was well used to women flattering him and being ostentatious in their desire for his comfort, but that was because it suited them to. All the ladies of his acquaintance, family or otherwise, had their own interests in mind. Catherine, astoundingly, seemed to be in earnest. 'You are forgetting the furniture to move,' he said gravely. 'Are the bedchambers on this floor or do we go up one more?'

'They may be on this one as we are in the country now.'

But the first door Nick opened was a large salon fronting the house. 'There will be some at the back almost certainly, but up again will be quickest. We can explore properly tomorrow.'

'Not how you expected to spend your Sunday,' said Catherine with a rueful smile.

And if anyone had told him he was looking forward to the novelty, he'd have had them committed. 'A change is as good as a rest, as my nanny used to say. What she meant, I suspect, was that

44

by sending me to the stables in charge of the groom for a change, *she* could have her rest.'

A burst of laughter escaped from her. As in the carriage, the gentle light from the candle made her face seem less drawn, more like a young woman ought to be. How old was she? Twenty-five? She seemed nearer his own age of thirty by daylight. 'Here we are,' she said, rounding the top of the newel post. 'Pick a room, Ann.'

The first room was small, with a single window and a narrow bedstead to match. A valet's room, or a maid's, Nick deduced. The second chamber had a bigger bed and was much larger, though similarly uncurtained. 'In here will do for Ann and me for tonight,' said Catherine, glancing around. 'God knows, we are used to moving, but I don't want her alone on the first night in a new place.'

'I'll take the first room, then.' But Nick paused, seeing the little girl's face fall. Of course, the valet's room would have been exactly the right size for a child. 'Unless there is another further along with more space for my . . . for my clothes?'

Immediately, Ann darted to the third door and looked inside. 'This one does! There is a closet *and* a big bed.'

He sketched a bow to her. 'Far more suited to my dignity. Not to mention my accoutrements. Thank you.'

The little girl giggled, then clapped a hand over her mouth, her eyes scared in case she had offended him. He winked and ruffled her hair, remembering all the times he had been given an icy stare for stepping out of line while he was growing up.

Catherine fixed her daughter with a look. 'You are still sleeping with me tonight. I'm too tired to get lost finding the door to your room when you wake.' She glanced up gratefully at Nick. 'That was kindly done. Thank you.'

Just for a moment, warmth ran through him like a sip of the best French brandy. If he was not careful, mother and daughter alike were likely to undo him.

'Bags,' he said abruptly. 'And bedding. And then, perhaps, a slice of that pie.'

3

Kitty's eyes snapped open. Why was it so quiet? What had happened? Her heart rate increased, feeding her alarm. Then she registered the light filtering through the square panes of an unfamiliar window. Of course. She was no longer in London. She was in Furze House at the top of the High Street in Newmarket, not four miles from where — many lifetimes ago, it seemed — she had grown up. She put out a hand and felt Ann sleeping beside her, as safe as any six-year-old could be.

Kitty made herself stay where she was, though the urge to dart from the bed to check the window closures and the door bolts was almost overpowering. She took a long breath, and then another, before sliding quietly out from between the sheets. Ann deserved this untroubled rest. Her existence so far had been all caution.

She looked out of the window at a peaceful workaday scene: hens pecking on the drive, a horse and groom trotting along the High Street towards the heath, a covered cart heading the other way into town, and the wide East Anglian sky surmounting the whole. This was the start of their new life. She was going to embrace it and make it work. Concentrate on *now*, that was the way of it. Make every minute her own, not someone else's. And push well to the back of her mind the possibility that Flint may be looking for her to snip off a loose end of thread.

★   ★   ★

Nicholas Dacre looked at the sky through the dusty window for some time before he moved. He felt odd; not just cold, though it was certainly that in this bare room without even a fire to take the edge off the day. No, he felt . . . different. Alert. Similar to walking on to the fencing floor to face an unknown opponent. A sense that, for once, he did not know what the day would bring. It was as if he'd stepped into a new skin. If he'd been closer to his portmanteau, he'd have reached for a mirror to check his reflection was still the same.

It was, naturally, all nonsense. This clarity of mind was probably induced by the vigilance of the journey, that heart-stopping moment when Catherine had nearly been seen at the inn in Hatfield and the breathtaking solution she had found, and then the unaccustomed hard work of hauling the carriage inside the barn before anyone glimpsed it on the Furze House drive.

He sat up, noting with astonishment the novel sensation of having a clear head. It was the first night in years he had slept without recourse to the bottle. Perhaps that was the reason for this alertness. Or maybe it was simply that he was cold and hungry. He trod quietly over to the window, checked all was undisturbed outside, and pulled a quilted robe out of his valise. They'd left the hamper in the sitting room. Hopefully there was also a log basket and kindling by the grate.

As he stepped into the passage, the next door along opened. Catherine slipped through it, dark hair loose, blue robe wrapped around her, her eyes wary.

Nick leashed the instant attraction that took hold of him. He was supposed to be protecting her. They needed to keep relations between them on a business-like basis. 'Good morning,' he said. 'I was just about to investigate the firewood.'

'And I the possibility of hot water,' she said. Her voice was low. She glanced into the room behind her and pulled the door quietly closed. 'Ann is asleep still. The silence woke me. It is so different to Covent Garden.'

'Will you adapt?'

'Oh yes. I could wish Verity had warned me a little more about what to expect, but I daresay she had no idea herself. It matters not. I have created enough homes out of nothing that this is a palace.'

'A cold one. An ice palace.'

She slanted an amused look at him. 'If you are thinking to remedy that by investigating the woodpile, you may need to modify your costume.'

'And you do not?'

'I am assuming there will be sufficient for a kitchen fire tucked under cover in the scullery. No cook would neglect such a thing, even if the household was packing up to leave the next day.'

'Is that so? I shall remember in future. I was thinking more of log baskets.'

'Each to their calling. Are you regretting your lack of valet now?'

'My valet would have cut me loose and been on the night mail back to London as soon as we arrived. Are you thinking I cannot lay a fire? I assure you, no one brought up in my grandfather's household is any stranger to the craft. We couldn't be, not if we wanted to survive the winter. If we were not bothered enough to learn, evidently we didn't feel the cold. He believes in toughening up his descendants.'

'Then I shall glean some knowledge from you. My proficiency, such as it is, is entirely self-taught.'

They had descended to ground level by this time. Catherine walked past the sitting room. Nick thought regretfully of the picnic hamper as he followed her towards the back of the house.

'A baize door,' he said. 'My second-favourite place after the stables when I was a boy.'

'Food?'

'Food, warmth, a place where I could be myself.' He stopped, startled. What was he about, saying so much to her? It must be the dressing robes and the silent house and the sense of adventuring together. It gave him the feeling they were comrades. This was unnerving. He didn't have women friends.

Acquaintances, yes — any number of them. Carefully selected lovers, all players in Society's game. Friendship was reserved for a few trusted men.

Catherine pushed open the door to the servants' passage, her robe making an interesting movement as it clung briefly to her legs before swirling free again. Nick drew a careful breath. He definitely didn't feel this way towards any of his male friends.

A sudden loud crash came from the door at the far end. Even before his next breath, he'd pulled Catherine to his side. 'Housebreakers,' he said. 'Stay here while I disarm them.'

★   ★   ★

Kitty had just been thinking how odd it was simply to be friends with a man, when the crash of a coal scuttle from the kitchen made her jump and Nicholas's instinctive shielding motion woke her body up and sent all kinds of disturbing signals through it. 'Disarm them with what, your dressing robe belt?' she said caustically. 'Don't be foolish. Listen.'

They heard a woman's voice raised in imprecation. 'Look at my floor. What are they going to think? You sweep that up.'

'The gardener and his wife,' said Nicholas, relaxing his hold.

Kitty was very much aware of him; his muscles, the scent clinging to his quilted robe. Also his unthinking assumption that he was there to protect her. That was an entirely new phenomenon and one it would be wise not to become accustomed to. 'This is my part to play,' she murmured, and stepped around him to push open the kitchen door.

'Good morning, Mrs Green,' she said. 'You are up very early.'

There was a squawk. 'Mum.'

Kitty took one look at the defensive face and knew the line to take. She had been in desperate situations too often herself not to recognise mute appeal in someone else. 'Oh, how very kind of you,' she said with warm appreciation. 'I came down to coax a fire into life for washing water and maybe a hot drink, but I see you are before me. I wonder . . . is it too much to hope that you might be able to do the same every morning?'

Relief shone out of the woman. 'I'd be glad to, mum, and I've got a niece lives with us what can do floors and fires. She's slow, like, but willing.'

'That's settled then. It will save me the trouble of finding anyone and you will both be a great help to me. We will come to some arrangement about payment when I see what else might need putting in hand. Circumstances have changed since my sister took the house. She is to be married, and my mother also, so they will not always be here. I am to keep house for them. My friend and her mother are to open a laundry at the back and we will be taking in respectable lady lodgers. Any gentlemen friends of Mr Congreve, such as Mr Dacre who was so kind as to bring Ann and me in his chaise yesterday, will stay in the other wing.'

Mrs Green looked doubtful. 'That's scarce ready for company, mum.'

'Then he must continue in the main house for the time being. If I could just take a couple of cans of water for now?'

'Yes, mum, the fire's drawing nicely. It won't be the work of a moment.'

'And you must tell me at what hour the service at St Mary is this morning.'

'Eight o'clock, mum. Reverend always has it early when the meetings are on, on account of . . . on account of . . . '

'On account of the racing gentlemen not all being as reliably pious as one might wish,' finished Kitty. She exchanged a look with Mrs Green in which each understood the other perfectly. 'Very well, I'll take the cans of water up, and you and I will talk later, or perhaps tomorrow. My thanks for your thoughtfulness this morning.'

'You did that very nicely,' said Nicholas as they carried their prize back up the stairs. She hadn't demurred as he relieved her of his own can. She was simply grateful he'd stayed out of Mrs Green's range of vision. The sight of his lean, dangerous good looks in that quilted robe did not at all accord with the idea of a respectable house guest.

'The poor woman was terrified we would have a full complement of staff to push her out of a job and out of their cottage.'

'As it is, you have no one.'

'You are forgetting my circumstances. I need very little. Cooking I can do myself and by the end of two or three weeks, the others will be here. If I am not using all the rooms, I do not need to clean them or heat them. The kitchen, these bedchambers and that pretty sitting room will be ample.'

He raised his eyebrows. 'No dining parlour? You think to eat in the kitchen?'

'It is likely to be the warmest room in the house. We could move a work table into the sitting room and use that if you prefer. Would that better suit your dignity?'

'I am open to fresh experiences. Speaking of which, if you really intend on going to church, I should accompany you.' His tone held a hint of long-suffering, no doubt hoping she would think better of her decision. He was out of luck. This was her new life and it did not include being told what to do by gentlemen who were in no way related to her.

'There is no need. Ann and I will be perfectly safe. Did you not hear Mrs Green? The service is timed so the racing fraternity are unlikely to disturb the peace of the churchgoers.'

'It is not them I am concerned with. Have you forgotten yesterday so soon? You may yet be hunted by Flint or his agents. You had best keep close to the buildings or hedges and I will obscure you as far as possible by walking on your other side. If it comes to it, I can fight off attackers.'

Kitty felt her stomach twist. She *had*

forgotten. The pull of safe childhood haunts had dulled her reflexes. 'That is very chivalrous of you. Fighting is the one thing I cannot do. Gentlemen are strong and able to deal with possible molesters. Women are at a disadvantage.'

He paused on the stairs. 'I was not always strong,' he said. 'I spent much time laid up as a child. However, there are ways in which even a sickly reed of a boy may overpower an opponent for long enough to make his escape. A bullying cousin, for example. It is a question of applying leverage. If you wish it, I could teach you.'

Kitty's breath caught in her throat. To have the ability *not* to be subject to any man's passing whim. To be confident of having enough skill to fight back without fear of reprisal. 'Yes,' she said. 'Yes, and yes again. Thank you.'

Meeting his gaze was a mistake. His eyes were dark and warm with a troubled relief at the back of them that said rather more about his interest in her than she was prepared to credit on so short an acquaintance. She suspected the mock love-making in the coach yesterday had been a mistake.

'But not now,' he said abruptly. 'There is scarce time to get washed and dressed before setting out for the church service as it is.'

★   ★   ★

Whatever Nicholas's design, it was regrettably pleasant to be escorted to church by a gentleman who was well dressed without trying, and who was solicitous of her and Ann as a matter of course. As he deftly steered them around a hole imperfectly filled with loose stones and dirt, Kitty tried to despise herself for enjoying the attention, but couldn't. She realised all over again how Simon had always *looked* the gentleman, but true manners had not been bred into his bones as they had with Nicholas Dacre.

'You do not have to come inside with

us,' she said. 'I am persuaded you will be very bored.'

'As well be bored inside as out,' he said. 'And once I am within, there will be no one to see me and wonder at my sudden ecclesiastical leanings.'

'Oh,' she said, stricken. 'That is true. You are not supposed to be acting out of the ordinary. You had best go back to Furze House directly.'

'I was jesting. The likelihood of any of my acquaintance being up at this hour is remote. If they are, I shall say I was out early to check on my riding horse.'

Kitty glanced at him with a frown. 'We travelled in your carriage. There was no riding horse that I saw.'

'Not on this occasion, but surely you remember there are three October meetings in Newmarket.'

'Why yes, my father used to go to them all, but I do not quite see . . . '

'The meetings on the heath are best attended on horseback. My groom brought Satan up at the end of

September for that purpose. He has been eating his head off in livery this past month.'

Kitty stared ahead, words deserting her. A month at livery, simply so Nicholas could watch the racing in style? Truly this man belonged in a different world. It was not even the one she used to belong to; the careless squandering of wealth both appalled and fascinated her. Fortunately Ann created a distraction by shyly saying how she loved Fred Grimes's patient old mare, but horses were very *big*, weren't they? Nicholas made the child laugh with a tale of the time he had fallen off his first pony, which had seemed huge to him at the time, but which was probably only half the size of the horses he rode now.

We inhabit different worlds. It was a salutary reminder. For all she had once been a gentleman's daughter, it would do Kitty no good to become accustomed to Nicholas Dacre's presence. It would certainly not do to become fond of him. He was here for the week and would then be gone. Back to his proper sphere.

They reached St Mary's church without incident. Kitty added her voice to the hymns, let the correct responses return to her lips and tried to feel morally uplifted and virtuous. That she was not entirely successful, she put down to Nicholas choosing to sit next to her, rather than on the other side of Ann as she had intended. It was distracting having his nankeen-clad thigh pressed against hers; she couldn't help recalling those moments in the carriage and his protective hold in the kitchen passage.

There was a flurry at the door. Kitty felt Nicholas's muscles instantly turn to steel, ready to fight. Her heart thumped at the sudden change, at the menace he projected. Was it Flint? Had he found her so soon? As the congregation turned to see what was happening, she shrank back, peering around Nicholas's taut body just long enough to spot a stout townswoman, red-faced and embarrassed at her late arrival, sinking hastily on to a bench.

The congregation returned its attention to the pulpit, Nicholas relaxed and Kitty breathed again, but her skin was clammy and when she clasped her hands in prayer, her pulse beat rapidly against her palm. It was borne in on her that the flight from London had given her the mere illusion of safety. She could not continue like this. For the remainder of the service, though she appeared to listen, her thoughts were given to something else entirely.

The rector — ever eager to expand his flock — exchanged a few words with her and Ann on the way out, welcoming them to Newmarket and enquiring if Kitty was making a prolonged stay in the town. She felt Nicholas's movement of annoyance when she explained she was the new housekeeper at Furze House.

'It is of no use stiffening up like that,' she observed as they walked back along the lane between the church and the high street, with Ann copying the other children and jumping into drifts of copper-coloured fallen leaves from the hedge. 'I am what I am, and very grateful to be so. Ann, do please try to stay clean for the next ten minutes. You may get as dusty as you like exploring when we are home. And wait for us when you get to the corner. I want to be able to see you.'

'Yes, Mama,' sang Ann, jumping into another drift.

Home. There she went again, calling Furze House home. If it was to remain so, she must tackle this issue head-on. 'It is not yet over, is it?' she said.

Nicholas didn't pretend not to know what she meant. He shot a faintly ironic look at her. 'That was what I was trying to infer this morning.'

'I apologise. It took the disturbance at church to make me see it. Nothing happened, but I was agitated the whole time afterwards that it might.' She lowered her voice further. 'You will think me very ungrateful, but I cannot live like this. I thought all I wanted was for us to be safe, but hiding in the shadows forever, fearful that at any minute Ann may be snatched from me or worse . . . it is insupportable.'

There was sympathy in his voice as he said, 'No, it is not much of a life. It may be better to move to somewhere you have no connections at all.'

She kept her eyes on Ann, now hopping from foot to foot at the top of the lane where it met the High Street. 'I want to stay here. Newmarket is my home. But I will not wait tamely for Flint or his vassals to hunt for me.' She took a deep breath. 'I am going to hunt for *him.*'

Nicholas stopped for a moment in sheer amazement, then he strode to catch up with her. Kitty noticed that as he rounded the corner, his gaze skimmed each passer-by for potential trouble. 'But we have just *come* from London,' he said. 'My task is to keep you safe *here*, however much we might both prefer to be more active. Charles and Fitz and the rest of the Pool are casting the net in town.'

'You misunderstand me. My hunt would take place in Newmarket.'

'My brain is clearly addled. This is what a diet of sermonising before breakfast does for a man. Remind me to persuade you against the idea next Sunday. Explain this idea of yours to me please, for you are making no sense.'

'I have scarce worked it out myself,' confessed Kitty. 'It came to me in church. It is to be hoped that the Reverend repeats his sermons, by the by, for I did not hear one word today.'

'You missed very little, I assure you.'

In front of them, Ann crouched to make friends with a thin black cat who had ventured out from the archway of the White Hart. This was how a child should be, hopping, jumping into piles of leaves, sitting down anywhere to pet animals, free from worry or caution. For her daughter's sake, Kitty had to be rid of the menace oppressing them. 'I am being serious. I did not listen to the sermon, because I was thinking — and it occurred to me that there is something we can do.'

She had his attention now. 'We?'

She gave him a quick smile. 'Yes, for I do not believe I can succeed without help. Your reasoning is that I am in danger in Newmarket because Flint knows where my family lives and thinks I may return.'

'Yes.'

'He knows about me, because seven years ago he sent Simon to Kennet End to blackmail my father.'

'Yes.'

'Where did he get the information?'

Nicholas stopped for a second time. 'I beg your pardon?'

Kitty spoke slowly, validating her thought processes to herself. 'The note Simon secreted in my cookery book made one thing plain. Seven years ago, Flint knew that thirteen years before *that*, my father had paid a highwayman to kill Will Lawrence. Papa did it because Mr Lawrence was Anne Harrington's betrothed and he wanted to marry Anne himself. Which he did, and she became my stepmama.'

'You told me this on the journey yesterday. I fail to see . . . '

'How did he know, Nicholas? How did Flint know my father had made this dreadful bargain?'

'From your father himself?'

'Never. And also . . . ' She raised her voice. 'Ann, leave the cat alone, we are not adopting him. I am sure he has mice and to spare at the inn.'

Ann sighed and walked on ahead, drooping as only a six-year-old can manage.

'I daresay Furze House has mice too,' offered Nicholas as they both watched the cat follow her.

She rested her arm on his unthinkingly. 'It had best be a good hunter then, for I am not feeding it. There is only the game pie and the end of a piece of beef left and not so very much of either after last night. You had better take your meals at one of the inns today.'

'It would be wise to show my face at several of them. How do you know your father didn't tell Flint? What were you about to add?'

'I remembered something from when we were talking about Simon seducing those poor, wretched girls. Mama said my father was very pleased with Simon when he first came into the district. It was only later that Papa took violently against him, calling him a snake. Afterwards, he did calm down, but he was still cool in dealings with him. Naturally, in my eyes, that made Simon only the more desirable.'

Nicholas knit his brows. 'The inference being that at first your father had no suspicions, then Captain Eastwick broke the news to him that he had to buy Flint's silence. You are sure your father wouldn't have boasted about it to anyone before that? It is a long time to keep silent. At the races after a big win and rather too much brandy in consequence, perhaps?'

'Papa was not like that. He liked to be seen as an upstanding landowner. What sort of conversation could he possibly have that would involve the scandalous tale of a contract for murder?'

'I take your point, but if Flint did not get his knowledge from your father, then where? From the villain? Or maybe Flint himself was the highwayman. He is ruthless enough.'

They had reached Furze House. Ann and the cat were happily engrossed with each other on the doorstep. Kitty bit her lip. This was what was important: keeping Ann safe. She would fight for it as long as there was breath in her body.

'I hadn't thought that far. Knowing how Flint discovered Papa's secret comes at the end of the story. I couldn't track that from here. What I was wondering was how my father found the highwayman in the first place. How did he even know there would be a highwayman for hire? One cannot simply place an advertisement for a murderer as one might for a footman or a maid-of-all-work. There must have been an intermediary. Someone he knew must have told him the way of it. That is what I thought I might try to find out.'

He looked at her in astonishment. 'How?' he asked.

'It would have been someone local. He went nowhere other than here or Bury St Edmunds. Finding that person might lead to the man who killed Mr Lawrence. Once you have him, you and your friends might then track Flint.'

'Have you taken leave of your senses? You cannot go around Newmarket enquiring how best to remove someone from society with no questions asked!'

Kitty had realised that immediately. It was a question of waiting for him to see the answer. 'Women gossip,' she said. 'I daresay when Molly arrives, she will speedily discover the right sort of people to ask.'

'And if you find them, it will get back to Flint faster than a galloping horse.' He gave her an exasperated look. 'I am trying to keep you *safe*.'

Bless the man. He would reason soon enough that a gentleman would always have more success than a lady in sniffing out these things. He would doubtless then forge ahead without telling her. 'Well then,' she said, 'we must hope Papa wrote it down somewhere.'

'And you think such a record will still be at Kennet End six months after he died?'

She looked at him meditatively. 'It is possible, yes. My brother John is no reader. He has the least curious mind of anyone I have ever come across. He will have been exercised a great deal by the affairs of the estate since he succeeded to it. If he uses the desk in Papa's study at all, it will only be to look over the account books or impress any visitors. I would not put money on him spending a great deal of time in there. Why, I daresay he does not even know of the desk's hidden compartment.'

Nicholas stared, then threw back his head and gave an enormous laugh that had his shoulders shaking with mirth. Ann scrambled up, wide-eyed with surprise at this transformation. Kitty could hardly blame her. It was breathtaking.

'You little witch,' he said. 'And to think I was worried about being bored.'

He unlocked the door and went jauntily inside, every line of him delighted. Ann followed. Kitty stood rooted to the spot, too transfixed even to make an attempt at stopping the cat from trotting after her daughter.

Simon had laughed a lot. But never *with* her like that. Never with approval. And certainly never as if she had just said something marvellous and amusing and all the things she knew she was not.

She unstuck her feet and went indoors. This, she thought, her pulse fluttering like a schoolgirl's, was going to take some dealing with.

4

Considerably happier with the prospect of something productive to do, rather than kicking his heels waiting for trouble to find them, Nick changed into less restrictive clothes, left Catherine and her daughter at Furze House and retraced his steps to the White Hart. There he did justice to a hearty breakfast and followed it with some time in the stables with his groom and the carriage horses.

'You'll not be taking them out today?' said this individual. It was more of a statement than a question.

'No, I'm off to turf Thomson from his cosy roost and take Satan on the heath for a spell. You're comfortable here?'

'Snug enough. I take it I'm not to know where you're staying?'

'You take it correctly. You may be as

stupid as you choose, but not so stupid as to neglect to find out who's asking.' Nick clapped the man on the shoulder, brushed a wisp of straw from his buckskins and headed for the livery stables.

Satan was fresh and took all his concentration for the first half-hour, which was just the way he liked it. As he finally eased back on the reins, he felt the cares return to his head. He hadn't expected one exhilarating ride to banish them — it never did — but he did feel better able to examine them now. Or to examine one of them at least.

Kitty Eastwick, now Catherine Redding. She was such a mixture of parts. Quiet and watchful, yet with an unexpected sense of humour and that breath-snatching layer of passion not far beneath the surface. And beautiful, and brave, and . . . and intelligent and caring. In short, she was the most tempting woman to have strayed across his orbit in a very long time and he wasn't entirely sure how to keep her at arm's length.

With Satan safely stowed, Nick was

strolling along Newmarket High Street when he felt an overly-familiar hand on his shoulder.

'Dacre, you sly fox. Where have you been hiding yourself?'

'Hardly hiding, Perry. I've been in the stables and on the heath. Where else would I be?'

'Tucked up with your ladybird, that's where. And don't say you haven't been, because I saw you both from my window this morning.'

Nick cursed silently. He'd known going to church was a mistake. They'd only passed one hotel, but that had apparently been enough. Viscount Perivale must be staying at the White Hart. He put on an expression of mild concern. 'Are you feeling quite the thing, Perry? One too many last night, perhaps? I freely admit enjoying the favours of a very affectionate lady on my way here, but I don't commonly mix women with racing. Priorities, you know.'

'Doing it too brown. You're devilish recognisable, Dacre.'

Nick shrugged. If he argued, Perry would only ferret harder until he had incontrovertible evidence. 'My valet will be delighted to hear it. By the by, I've been meaning to ask — why the green ribbons?'

Viscount Perivale glanced down at his boots, where emerald green ribbons had been knotted around the tassels. 'Oh, I'd forgotten them. I've a bet on with Jack Feathers. He wagered I could wear 'em for a month and no one would notice. I said people would. He's written down how many people he thinks will ask what it's about and lodged it at Whites. I mark off how many people actually mention them. If I get more than he's written down, he gives me a monkey.' He fished out a pocket book and a stub of a pencil. 'You make one more for the tally. Mighty obliged to you. May as well see who's in the coffee house, eh?'

As this was precisely where Nick had been heading, he was forced to change his plans. He had no wish to be the butt of Perry's humour for the rest of the morning. 'I'll be in later. I'm meeting a couple of fellows at the Rutland Arms.' He lifted a hand in farewell and strode off.

In the coffee lounge of the Rutland he discovered several acquaintances ensconced around a card table. From the sallies he received, he gathered that the story of his supposed amorous encounter in Hatfield was already known.

'Perry said he didn't know where to put his face,' guffawed one gentleman.

'If he'd kept it out of my private carriage, he wouldn't have had the problem,' replied Nick without heat. 'He was on about it again this morning. Matter of fact, I didn't think he seemed too well. Going it yesterday, was he?'

There was another ripple of laughter. 'I'll say. Lord knows where he got the blunt. He hadn't a feather to fly with a couple of days ago.'

Nick nodded in an uninterested fashion, called for a tankard of ale and settled down to peruse the *Racing*

Calendar ahead of the week's meetings. He'd realised years ago that the less you made of something, the sooner it would sink out of sight of the collective consciousness.

When he finally returned to Furze House, he found his passage down the hallway barred by a moderately-sized table resting on its side, half in and half out of the sitting room.

'I appear to be just in time,' he murmured, and laying a finger on his lips to enjoin Ann's silence, he hoisted the legs that the child was trying to lift.

'Goodness, that's better,' said Catherine's voice from behind the door. 'Well done, Ann. How did you manage to . . . ? Oh, Mr Dacre, thank you. We were going on very nicely but this door is most unfortunately positioned close to the wall, so we were obliged to angle the table all the way around.'

Nick surveyed the sitting room, noting with amusement the black cat curled into a corner of the sofa. 'You have made this room charming. You would like the table next to the window, I take it?'

'For the moment, yes. Ann and I discovered it in a large parlour which held nothing else at all. It was most disconcerting. No doubt it will prove to be infested with woodworm, and will stealthily destroy all the furnishings in this room too.'

A bubble of laughter rose in Nick's chest. 'You seem very sanguine about the prospect.'

She waved an airy hand. 'I no longer concern myself with anything too far in the future. For now, this room is pretty and functional, I have prepared a fricassee with the remnants of the hamper and I have had a profitable talk with Mrs Green regarding eggs. I have met her niece Eliza who is good at floors and fires, I know that the best butcher is still to be found in the Market Square, that there is a very good fish stall in the market on Thursdays and a coal office on the High Street. Oh, and for a very reasonable sum, Mr Green is to supply us with vegetables in season either of his own growing or by some arcane bartering system with his cronies.'

'You have been busy to some purpose. I feel disgustingly idle having merely exercised my horse, shown my face around the town and sown the seeds of doubt about Viscount Perivale's cognitive capacity. Tell me, with what will Mr Green barter?'

'I thought it wisest not to ask. I *was*, however, enjoined not to heed any comings or goings after dark on a Sunday, as it is only his group and nothing to worry my head about and if anyone *should* start to sing, it will be most respectful.'

The laugh could be contained no longer. It burst from Nick's throat. 'After that, I am minded not to stir from the house for the rest of the day and instead set up a watching station from an upper window.'

'You should be minded to behave exactly as you would normally.'

'I have been doing so, and been well roasted for my pains. What other treasures have you found here?'

There was a tiny pause. 'Firewood. A better table service than the one we used last night. Sufficient pots and knives that the kitchen is functional. We thought to ensure the basic necessities first, before seeking out treasures.'

'I did find the spice box, Mama.'

Catherine smiled down at her daughter. 'You did. Treasure indeed. The most beautiful inlaid box, Nicholas, tucked into a blanket chest for safe-keeping with the key still in the lock. Someone is no doubt even now grieving over its loss. Ann will show it to you. Do you care to take an inventory of the rest of the house with us?'

Ann wriggled off the sofa expectantly. The cat stretched in a casually disinterested fashion.

Looking at the child's eager face, Nick abandoned his notion of sleeping for the afternoon. 'Certainly. I should be glad of a night-stand if one can be found. Does the cat come with us?'

Catherine slanted him a resigned look. 'Apparently, yes.'

Nicholas made an unexpectedly good surveyor, thought Kitty. He produced a pocket book and a pencil and took notes as they went from room to room. They decided unanimously that the superior rear bedchambers on the first floor should be kept for Verity and Mrs Bowman when they were in Newmarket, and instead carried extra pieces from unused second floor rooms into their own to make them complete.

It amused Kitty that Nicholas knew exactly what he needed. For all his talk of firecraft, this was a man accustomed to the best. She was less diverted by his frowning observation that her room seemed very sparse. It was easier to agree to the addition of a small table and chair by the window than it was to tell him she required nothing more. It also kept him interested in cataloguing the house. She hadn't been wholly truthful when she'd said she and Ann had been too busy seeing to their comfort downstairs for anything else. Ann had been desperate to explore, but all the empty rooms unnerved Kitty. Once she would have thought nothing of having so much space about her, but that was before she had spent seven years making tiny nests amongst the seething humanity of the streets.

The top floor disclosed a network of smaller rooms, some with furniture, some without. Their footsteps echoed on the wooden boards. 'You will be able to accommodate several lodgers,' said Nicholas, uncannily mirroring her thoughts.

'I shall be glad of it.' At his look of surprise, she went on haltingly. 'Not just for the rent. I have become used to having people living on either side of me. Noise above. Noise below. It is so quiet here I am jumping at the least sound.'

He was silent for a moment. 'My grandfather's house is rarely empty, but you are talking about something different, I think.'

She tried to explain. 'When I first came away with Simon, everything was strange to me. He used to go out for long periods and I was lonely. I had been used to sitting with Mama or Verity, writing letters, fashioning bonnets or sewing. In London I knew no one and could not simply stroll from room to room in search of diversion as I had at home because people were private and the apartments were separate. It was so very foreign. It was not until I absorbed the truth that everyone I could hear around me had their own story and their own struggles that I understood the comfort of being able to control my own living space, of being apart from the world, yet within it.'

He was frowning. 'You limited your expectations, in effect? Yes, I see.'

'Do you? In essence what I found was akin to the life of an entire country neighbourhood contracted down to one building, one courtyard. My own walls had to hold all my consolation. One small life, slotted in amongst other people's lives.'

He nodded slowly. 'And now you

miss those lives around you.'

'I confess I do.'

'You did well, I think. I cannot imagine many ladies of my acquaintance adjusting to such a drastic change. I must admit, an escape into anonymity sounds immeasurably desirable to me. You have no idea how I envy Charles Congreve his set of rooms in the Albany.'

There was a bleakness in his eyes that warned her off asking further. Was his home so very bad? Too formal, perhaps?

'I must write to Verity and ask if Charles can arrange the allowance he mentioned,' she said, changing the subject. 'It is all very well having this many rooms, but they are sadly lacking as far as potential occupiers are concerned. I cannot see the linen draper extending me credit for the curtaining I will need to buy for example, though I suppose I can dress the rooms one lodger at a time if needs must.'

'I can lend you money for day-to-day needs, and the Dacre name carries sufficient credit to open most accounts,' said Nicholas. 'If the Pool is to run Furze House, Benedict Fitzgilbert will fund the venture. I will speak to him when I am back in London.'

'That would be useful. Thank you. I hope it will not prove too expensive. Evidently whoever had the house last took all their bedchamber furnishings with them. I daresay the blankets Ann found were the ones provided originally with the house.'

Nicholas glanced up at the ceiling. 'I wonder . . . If you are minded to be frugal, there may be outmoded furnishings in the attics. Previous tenants may have stored old drapes up there. I know our attics in town are an Aladdin's cave of past fads. The Dacre women are not known for entertaining amongst last season's fashions.'

Kitty experienced another moment of shock. It had been so long since she'd thought of attics as anything but a source of cheap dwelling that she hadn't even considered discards. 'That is an excellent idea,' she said with enthusiasm. 'There must be a stair on this floor somewhere.'

Ann found the attic stair easily enough, concealed behind a door, but Kitty noticed she was flagging. 'One quick look, and then we will investigate the fricassee,' she promised.

Nicholas ascended first. She heard his snort of laughter. 'Prepare for disappointment. This is not so much an Aladdin's cave as a rag-and-bone man's yard. I defy you to find a sound item anywhere. In a positive light, I suppose we can always use the broken chairs for firewood.'

Kitty arrived beside him and surveyed the relics of the last fifty years with a rather more practical eye. *Firewood?* There spoke a man who had never needed to count every last farthing. 'You are too nice,' she said. 'Dusty they may be, but any carpenter will be able to mend these. I must ask Mrs Green when the chair-caning man visits the town. Why, there must be several rooms' worth. Can we stack them to one side perhaps? I think I see a large trunk by that joist.'

'So you do.' He cleared a passage to it and then with a mighty heave, freed the clasp and lifted the lid. 'Curtains. I was right. Treasure at the first hit. I hope you like pink and blue damask.'

'Yes! Oh, how wonderful. Aren't they pretty, Ann? And not very much faded at all. My congratulations on an excellent notion, Nicholas.'

Kitty left the curtains in her room, then bustled her daughter down to the kitchen to wash the dust off herself and feed her. She'd put the hangings up when they had eaten.

Nicholas hovered in the doorway. 'That smells very good. May I eat with you? Is there enough?'

Kitty tried to keep her surprise from showing. 'There is, though it is only the last scraps of the beef, together with some vegetables and onions and a pinch of cinnamon from Ann's spice box. Would you not prefer to dine with your friends in one of the hotels?'

'And be quizzed as to where I have been all afternoon? I shall have to go out later. Just now I am minded to be domestic.'

He looked so adrift with the concept that Kitty laughed. 'Were you never so before? You are welcome to stay, but I warn you it will be all in one dish, with the last of the bread dipped in.'

'I believe my sensibilities can cope.'

'Set another place then, Ann, and we will use the pretty plates. Why must you go out tonight? Is there a card game you are promised to?'

'Such a promise I could easily break. No, the *Magnet* gets in at two this morning from London. I have a fancy to see who gets off it.'

The pit of Kitty's stomach dropped away. She added a third plate to the table in a mechanical fashion. 'See what rummaging in attics does for the memory. My head is so full of curtains I had near forgotten potential spies. You think Flint may have sent someone by the mail coach?'

'It would be foolhardy to ignore the possibility. It is likely that any alighting passengers will be after nothing more than the race meeting, but it would be as well to be aware of them. I will try not to disturb you when I return.'

'Noise is unlikely to disturb me. It is the silence I cannot get used to.' She hesitated. 'You cannot keep watch on all the coaches. Several a day call here from London on their way to Bury St Edmunds or Norwich.'

'Flint works fast, in our experience. Tonight or tomorrow is more likely than the rest of the week to bring our man, if there *is* a man. I shall invent some sort of indisposition preventing me from attending the heath tomorrow and patrol the main street instead.'

A stab of guilt assailed Kitty that he was putting off his own pleasure in order to safeguard her. 'Something that allows you to leave the house but not ride? A sprained ankle?'

'That would answer. Though in all probability whoever it is will have already arrived by post-chaise and be ensconced in one of the inns.' He moved across the room and put a hand on her shoulder. 'I have upset you. I should not have mentioned it.'

His touch sent awareness racing through her. He was too near, too solicitous.

She whisked over to the range to bring the pan to the table. 'And leave me the worse prepared because you thought to spare me? I am not such a poor creature.' She glanced at Ann, sitting on the floor stroking the cat. 'Once, maybe. Not any more. Now, I prefer all my cards face-up.'

⋆　⋆　⋆

The simple meal was very good and Nick said so. 'I see now why you weren't worried about not having any domestic staff yet. Have you always cooked? Where did you learn? Did you escape to the kitchen at an early age as I did to the stables?'

A shadow crossed Catherine's face.

There was a smudge of flour on her forehead that he longed to brush off. 'I might have done before Papa remarried. I was very young. I do remember warmth and comfort and good smells. After he married again I was either in the nursery or with Mama. I didn't learn to cook until I came to London.' She shot him a quick glance, as if to see whether he was really interested or simply being polite.

'Go on,' he said.

'I told you Simon left me alone a great deal. Sometimes there was money when he returned, often there wasn't. We had been eating at the inn nearby. As the coins in my purse dwindled, I realised I would have to cook for myself. I had the *Domestic Cookery* book Mama had given me, but I didn't understand the instructions. What did 'put to the fire' mean, for example? What was a fore-quarter? Or a griskin? So I went across the courtyard to the inn kitchen and asked the cook there what it all meant.'

'Good heavens.' Nick's assessment of her character went up another notch.

'It was a busy inn and she was short of help. She wasn't going to turn down a free pair of hands. In return for chopping vegetables, she taught me how to make broth. In return for kneading pastry, she showed me how to make a pie. I found I enjoyed it. Cooking has its own alchemy: certain dishes need to be cooked fast, others are best when left to gather flavour for some hours. By the time we had to move to cheaper rooms, I knew enough to survive.'

She stood abruptly and started to clear the dishes. Nick waited for a moment, but the confidences were evidently at an end. He repeated his thanks for the meal and went outside for a breath of fresh air, feeling unsettled. What was the matter with him? Why should he feel inadequate because a woman he'd only met a day ago proved to be so unexpectedly courageous about facing challenges? He walked down towards the far end of the grounds. At home when he felt like this he headed for the fencing salon to work off his fidgets, but Newmarket didn't run to one. Was the stable block large enough that he could get in some practice by himself?

He executed a few limbering-up exercises and thought it was, so went back for his foil. Opening the door of his room, he was startled by the sight of Ann sitting cross-legged on his bed and Catherine balanced on his table with her arms full of pink and blue damask.

A wave of complete shame engulfed him as he realised he'd expected the drapes to appear at his window having been invisibly put up by servants. Had he been a quarter of an hour later in returning, he would have accepted their presence without question. But of course there *was* no one but Catherine to do it, and now he had startled her whilst attempting to hook up the pole on her own and she was overbalancing . . .

In two strides he was across the room and lifting her down. She was supple, yet tense in his arms, coiled steel wrapped in kidskin. 'Did you not think to ask for help?' he said, more roughly than he intended.

'I was perfectly safe,' she said, sounding breathless. 'And Ann did help by threading the rings on the pole.'

He let her go before he was too tempted to keep hold of her, and swung himself up to the table in her place. 'Tell me what to do,' he said. 'In simple terms as befits an idiot, please, for I have never hung curtains before.'

By the time they had completed all three of their rooms, the urge to fence had left him, though he got the foil out of its sheath and made a few practice passes to satisfy Ann. He rested on his bed instead, wondering at his confusion of mind and trying to forget the feeling of Catherine's light, taut body in his arms.

★   ★   ★

At one in the morning, Nick let himself quietly out of Furze House and strolled down the High Street. The moon gave him plenty of light to see where he was going, but even had there not been, the lit windows of the inns and hotels made it near as bright as St James's Street. Crockford's gaming house further down was decently closed — on the outside, at least — but for the rest, you'd never know it was the Sabbath. At Bottom's coaching office he passed a few words with the clerk then settled down in the shadow of the wall outside to wait.

He heard the horn being blown long before anything was visible, then the wildly dancing pinpricks of light hurtling down the road from the heath became four lanterns, the *Magnet* drew to a fast stop, disclosing another bright lantern to the rear, and the faintly green-looking passengers were forced to make haste and alight.

'Not so fast, give us a moment to fetch off the bags,' grumbled a large gentleman with a pronounced country drawl. 'You've fair shaken our insides to porridge.'

'You chose to travel by the Mail,' retorted the coachman. 'I can't idle here. I have to keep to the timetable.'

'On a moonlit night with an empty coach? You're talking through your hat, boy. You'll be so early at Thetford, you'll have to wait there ten minutes.'

While he was speaking, the outside passengers stumbled down from the roof. The remaining inside passengers were stamping their feet to keep warm as they waited for their luggage. By the time the large gentleman had finished his argument with the coachman, all the luggage was on the street.

'Thank you sir, thank you indeed,' said a thin, anxious-looking individual, bobbing his head at the countryman before hurrying up the road, a worn valise clutched under his arm.

Nick watched the other passengers — all of whom were familiar to him as race-goers — disappear in the direction of ale-houses or hotels. He gazed thoughtfully after the thin man.

'Forget him; he's an attorney's clerk,'

said the large gentleman without turning around. His country accent was noticeably less pronounced. 'On business for his master and taking the Mail for speed because his wife's sick. He was in a pother the whole way because on the last occasion, the coachman was so obsessed with keeping to the schedule that he didn't give everyone time to get the bags off. My little fellow had to chase after it halfway up the street.'

Nick grinned in the darkness and detached himself from the shadows. 'Adam Prettyman, I take it? I'm Nicholas Dacre. I met you in the fencing salon with Charles Congreve last month. I was expecting you tomorrow.'

Shrewd blue eyes sized him up. 'I remember you. I'm hoping you've got a mattress for me for the night. We thought it best to stagger our arrivals and I'd as lief not walk the three miles home after that hell-ride, especially as so much of it is wooded.'

Stagger arrivals? Who else was coming to Newmarket then? Nick hoisted one of Adam's bags. 'There's room and to spare. It's this way. We'll get a jug of ale from the White Lion. I'm not keen to be seen in the Hart this evening. Have you eaten?'

'They set me up with a piece for the road. You've had no trouble?'

A near sighting by Viscount Perivale, another scandal to add to my tally with my grandfather and an overwhelming urge to take the woman I am guarding to bed.

'Nothing we couldn't handle. Mrs Eastwick and the child have retired for the night. We are calling her Catherine here. Catherine Redding. A shipping clerk's widow.'

'That's prudent. I have a letter to her from Verity. She says she is to go to the Kennet End dower house and help herself to whatever is needed. There's also a letter from Mrs Bowman to the cook acquainting her with the changes and one to be delivered to her stepson whenever it is deemed most productive.'

Nick gave a soundless whistle. 'A letter for John Bowman? That could be very useful. I'll tell you why once we are indoors. What's the news from town?'

'Grosvenor Street is being watched. Verity is making a great fuss about searching for her sister. Charles has set Scrivener — a man he is known to use — to look for Catherine, and a rather more discreet fellow to observe anyone who tails Scrivener himself.'

'That would be helpful, if it works. Tracing anyone back to Flint is like trying to catch shadows in a net. Anything else?'

'The rooms they rented in Henrietta Street were ransacked before Eastwick's blood was even dry on the knife. It's set folk on edge. Catherine's friend Molly Turner is taking the long view and is on her way here tomorrow, with two of her children and her mother. Her son is following at hackney pace with a jarvey adoptee of Verity's. He's a friend of Molly's, I understand. He's bringing all their goods. There are two other women to come, but Charles has yet to arrange their release from the Bridewell.' He chuckled. 'Poor Charles. Another month and we won't recognise the man. My wife warned me how it would be. She calls it the Verity transfiguration.'

Nick remained unsympathetic. At least Charles had declared himself to Verity and been accepted. From where Nick stood, his friend was having it easy.

5

The drawback of a completely quiet house was that Kitty was abnormally aware of every new sound. There was a new sound downstairs now. She strained to hear. Nicholas was talking, but to who? Surely he hadn't enticed some dubious character back here to be questioned? The familiar feeling of not being in control crept over her. The desire to protect herself by shrinking into invisibility had her curling under the covers . . . No. She straightened abruptly. This was her new life. Grasp it, Kitty. Grasp it now.

She pulled on her wrap, lit a candle and made her way downstairs.

The sitting room fire had been coaxed back into life. Two men were sitting at the table, a jug of ale between them. They stood as she entered. Nicholas's eyes warmed with appreciation, recalling the very disturbing moment earlier when he strode across his room and grasped her firmly around the waist as she was measuring the height of his window. It had been quite unnecessary to lift her down, for she hadn't been in the least unbalanced, even if he had then climbed athletically to his table and made a far quicker job of sliding the curtain pole on to the brackets than she would have managed. Be that as it may, she flushed now at the memory of his arms close about her body and the flare in his eyes before he'd schooled his face to its normal noncommittal mask.

The man with Nicholas was a stranger. Or was he? Her sister's words came back to her. *A large, fair man with the kindest eyes ever.* 'Oh, are you Adam Prettyman?' asked Kitty. 'Verity told me you would be arriving on Monday, but I had not realised it would be so early.'

'Nor I,' said Adam with feeling. 'Let me tell you, Mrs Redding, the London mail coach is not an experience I am desirous of repeating.'

Mrs Redding. Nicholas had related her new history then. She glanced at him and he moved across to her.

'Sit down by the fire before you catch a cold. That robe is ridiculously thin.'

Then warm me. For a quite dreadful moment, Kitty thought she had said the words aloud. It must be because she was still half asleep. She hastily tucked herself into a corner of the sofa and listened while Adam told her all he had already said to Nicholas.

'Molly arrives tomorrow?' she said, dismayed. It was not that she didn't wish to see her friend, but nothing was ready for them. She had thought to have several days yet. Why would she come so early?

'By the afternoon coach, if tickets can be got. Verity may write more of the matter.' He felt inside his coat and handed her several letters.

When Kitty saw the one addressed to her brother John, she caught her breath. It would make the perfect excuse to call at Kennet End — but only if he was absent. She hurriedly scanned Verity's letter. 'My sister says the enclosure to John announces Verity's forthcoming nuptials, but not Mama's, due to Charles not quite having finalised getting a settlement from him in exchange for Mama giving up the dower house. So we must not mention that about the town.' She tapped John's letter, then looked up to meet Nicholas's eyes. 'I wonder if my brother spends as much time at the races as my father was wont to do?'

He grinned. 'It would be remarkably useful if he did.'

Adam nodded. 'Nick told me your idea of tracing a line back to Flint from how he knew of your father's crime. I'll ask in a discreet, roundabout fashion about assassins for hire. A former travelling player has access to lines of enquiry not in the common way.' He stifled a yawn. 'Do you have a mattress I might stretch out on for the rest of the night? I should like to get some rest before setting out for Rooke Hall. Jenny will be surprised to see me so early.'

Kitty raised her eyebrows. 'You will not be *that* early. If Molly and her mother are arriving tomorrow, the laundry will need clearing out. A man of your stature will be invaluable.' She rose to her feet. 'Pump in the scullery. Mattress upstairs in one of the rooms to the right of the stairs. Will you bank the fire, Nicholas? I will see you both in the morning.' *Assuming she could sleep with so many things to be done revolving in her head, and apprehension fluttering in her belly at the thought of what some of them might entail.*

★ ★ ★

Monday. Provisions first, before the town grew busy, and then cleaning. Kitty had little expectation that anyone would be watching for her this early, but took care to round her shoulders and pull her plain bonnet low on her head as she bought meat, bread and kitchen staples.

Nicholas, when she returned, did not see her reasoning in quite the same light. He burst out of the front door before she was a quarter of the way down the drive.

'Are you deranged?' he said in a tight voice. 'I am supposed to be guarding you. Can you imagine what has been going through my head since I came down and found you gone, with no note of explanation, and the side door unbarred?'

'It could not have been going through your head for long,' said Kitty, passing him on her way into the house. 'I have not been above twenty minutes and you were snoring when I left.' She didn't add that she had made as little disturbance as possible in order to avoid this very argument.

'I do not snore,' said Nicholas, outraged.

'No? Did Adam Prettyman then drag his mattress into your room?'

Kitty took her bonnet and shawl off and continued to the kitchen. He followed her, reaching to open the doors for her as they went.

'Thank you,' she said, caught unawares by the courtesy, and realised that even when he was wrathful, he kept it rigidly controlled within himself, rather than letting it rage on the surface. It made him difficult to read. It made him more complex and dangerous. Glancing at his shuttered face, she wasn't so very sure it was good for him. She began to unpack her basket, shivering a little as she put the milk on the cold stone floor of the pantry. 'I was not wholly irresponsible,' she said in a mild voice. 'Do you never speak to anyone not of your own class? Mrs Green is outside feeding her hens, and Mr Green is oiling the laundry doors. Both of them knew where I was going. I have bought oatmeal. Do you care for porridge for breakfast? I assure you it is not as horrid as it sounds if taken with a spoonful of honey, and you have no idea how far it stretches.'

'Catherine . . . ' He clenched his hands in frustration, clearly itching to shake some sense into her.

She put her hands on his to calm him, meeting his gaze squarely. 'I was careful. I did not draw attention to myself. This is an hour when many cooks and maids and the poorer townsfolk are doing their marketing. I blended in. I stood patiently in line. I bought the most economical cuts. I did nothing out of the ordinary. This . . . this slice of time is my world, Nicholas. It is the same in a market town as it is in London. I understand it. I am comfortable in it.'

He said, as if the words were being dragged out of him, 'It could not always have been so.'

'No indeed. But just because the reason I have learned stemmed from a lie, it does not mean I should forget the art now.' She tried a small smile. 'Especially when it is likely to be useful.'

To her relief, the tension leached out

of him. He gave a reluctant smile in return. 'I suppose it would be out of the question for a gentleman to accompany you at this hour?'

'Not unless you *wanted* to draw attention to me.'

'Then I must accept it, though I cannot help but be concerned.' There was a rueful expression in his eyes. 'You are wrong about one thing, Catherine: you will never be ordinary.'

'Why not? It is all I want to be, I assure you.'

He touched her cheek gently. 'With this face? With those eyes? You ask the impossible.'

She swallowed, unable to move. 'Then I must strive harder.'

Insensibly, imperceptibly, the air between them vibrated with heat. *I must stop this*, thought Kitty, then . . . *oh, was this why he'd been so cross?* 'No,' she said, the words already nearly beyond her. 'I would ruin you.'

'Also impossible,' he replied on an aching breath. His hand slid down, reaching for her.

The turning of the door handle shattered the moment. Kitty whirled around to plunge her hands in the basket, seeking the bread and the meat. Nicholas lurched towards the large kettle and swung it over to the range. When Ann danced in, with her black shadow at her heels and Adam following sleepily behind, Kitty was already reassuring her troublesome protector that she had, in fact, bought bacon as well as porridge with which to sustain him and that yes, she was putting it on a high shelf, well out of the range of any inquisitive cats.

★   ★   ★

That, thought Nick, regaining mastery of himself with a considerable effort, had been altogether too close. He continued to think it throughout breakfast, the investigation of the disused laundry and the sweeping out of a quantity of dust. Losing control then would have been a disaster. Only once over the years had he acted before thinking. That once had been a mistake so bitter it had coloured all his dealings with the female of the species since. Quite how Catherine Redding should have slipped under his guard he didn't know. She wasn't even trying to seduce him. A mocking inner voice pointed out that was probably the reason. He growled at it to be quiet. From now on, he vowed, he would keep his distance. He would bind up his ankle, spend the day limping along the High Street watching the various inns, and devote himself exclusively to male company.

The laundry proved to be one large room, two small ones above, and a tiny cottage crammed between it and the main house that did not look to have been used since the turn of the decade.

'There is little point clearing this,' objected Nick disparagingly. 'It is by far too small. Your friends would do better in the house.' *And with more people around, there was less chance of intimacy.*

Catherine spared him an unreadable glance. 'It is not too small for those accustomed to the Alsatia. The cottage will do very well with extra beds and a better table. Another set of drawers would be useful for the top room.'

'I need drawers too, Mama.'

Catherine dropped a kiss on top of her daughter's head. The casual affection between mother and daughter still took Nick by the throat and squeezed it. 'We will look as soon as you have clothes to fill it. Presently the bottom drawer of mine is more than sufficient, so little as we both have.' She looked around, distracted. 'I think they will have to use our kitchen until their goods arrive. We do not have enough utensils to divide up.'

'Molly Turner did not strike me as someone whom a visit to the ironmonger would put out of countenance,' said Nick. 'We are providing them with a house. It does not have to be perfect. You do not need to tease yourself so.'

'Yes I do,' she said, rounding on him

116

with startling fierceness. 'If Molly and her mother had not taken it upon themselves to look after me when I was close to term with Ann, we would likely both have died. Simon had left me near penniless in damp, louse-infested rooms while he went off to the country. He said he was going for work, but I know now it would have been to extort money from one of Flint's victims and almost certainly to seduce some gullible girl for himself while he was there. Don't you see? I would not have *survived* without the Turners. I owe them more than I can ever repay. Ma Turner was born in the country but Molly and the children have never lived out of London.' She gestured around her, encompassing the house, the heath beyond, and the wide open skies. 'Imagine all this through their eyes. Imagine how strange it will be for them. I *care* about them, Nicholas, and they are coming here because of me. I need to make their transition less ... less taxing.'

Nick stood, unable to move, appalled by the wrongness of his thinking. With one sentence she had turned all the lessons he had absorbed in his grandfather's house upside down. She was absolutely correct. He had been looking at this activity from a privileged position, not from the Turners' perspective at all. To his utter shame, it had not occurred to him that there *was* another perspective.

Adam had been quietly beating rugs free of dust and laying them back down. Now he said, 'There's a furniture broker in the High Street. Joseph Brasher. What he hasn't got in his barn, he'll be able to find you.'

'Thank you,' said Catherine. 'I must also remember to ask Mrs Green if she knows when the chimney in here was last swept or who might do it for us. I hope it will not be needed, for there is no faster way than a chimney sweep to spread the news that there are strangers in town.'

Nick was grateful for Adam's placid

intervention, but was chagrined that it had been necessary. He seemed to be wrong at every turn this morning. He might as well not be here. And now Catherine was looking at him, a crease of worry between her eyes as if she understood how much he was hating himself. He wasn't sure he could bear it.

She took a quick breath. 'Please don't rip up at me, Nicholas, but I have been thinking you should go to the heath as you would normally do when you are here for the horse racing. If anyone *is* in Newmarket from Flint, there should be nothing unusual for him to wonder at, however easily it can be explained.'

Having resolved earlier to keep his distance, Nick was immediately injured at being sent away. 'Then who will watch the stage arrivals? Who will meet your friend Molly and tell her where to go? *You* cannot be out in the middle of the afternoon for all to observe.'

'I will go,' said Adam, filling a pail of water from the pump. He gave Nick a look of masculine comprehension. 'I know, I know. You want to be doing something. Think, man, not drawing attention to yourself or Furze House is by far the best service you can do Catherine. Play to your strengths.'

'You must see it is true, Nicholas. You are easily the most suitable person to know who on the heath does not have their full attention on enjoying themselves,' cajoled Catherine. 'Or who is not there that you would expect to be present. You might even find out if anyone is asking questions about my brother. Or possibly you might see who he is in conversation with.'

'That is highly unlikely, as you would know if you had ever been to a Newmarket race meeting,' snapped Nick. 'The place is a mass of horseflesh and gentlemen hallooing to other gentlemen. Besides, how am I to know a man I have never seen in my life?'

Adam put down his pail, fished a scrap of paper from his pocket and sketched a brief outline of a man's face, heavy-set and pugnacious.

'That's John to the life,' cried Catherine. 'How clever you are.'

Jealousy roiled in Nick's stomach. 'I'd best get ready then,' he said ungraciously. He knew he was being unreasonable. Their suggestions made sense, but he didn't have to like the situation. He addressed Catherine with more force than he intended. 'One thing. Stay here at Furze House while I'm away. No more excursions like this morning.'

A tiny imp danced in the back of her eyes. 'Not even to the furniture broker with Adam?'

'Make a list,' he said through gritted teeth. 'I will call in with it and open us an account.' He paused. 'I need to know I can trust you.'

She relented, looking directly at him. 'Peace, Nicholas. I was teasing you. I will go nowhere else today. You can trust me. Let me heat you some washing water and find a stiff brush for your riding coat. You will not wish to attend the heath looking less than your best, I think? Ann, be very good for Adam, please.'

'We'll be grand,' said Adam. 'It's not so long since my Lottie was her age.'

★ ★ ★

I don't fit, thought Nick, striding irritably down the High Street a little later in search of Joseph Brasher's establishment. What was worse was that he didn't like the reason why. On the face of it, they were all three equal. Adam Prettyman was the younger son of a landed gentleman in Staffordshire. It was true he'd spent time as a touring actor, but he was now returned to the gentry. Catherine had been a gentleman's daughter before she eloped to London with her blackguard of a husband. With both of them Nick could converse on equal, amicable terms. Yet they slotted easily into this make-do, servant-free life as if they'd been born to it and he . . . he did not. They had

122

adapted because they had found themselves with nothing. Nick had never had nothing. The one time it had been threatened, he had capitulated. He didn't think he had ever hated himself more.

Voices jeered in his head. *Do you never talk to anyone not of your own class?* That was what Catherine had said this morning. She hadn't meant it as anything but a mild reproof, but it had sent him into such a defensive parry that he'd let slip control over his baser nature and had damn near ravished her there and then. It was unforgivable.

Do try to remember what you owe to your blood, Nicholas. Those had been his grandfather's cutting words when he'd innocently asked their attorney's pretty daughter to dance at the Christmas ball, the year he'd turned fifteen. Thereafter he *had* always remembered what was owed to his name, and much good had it done him. One more bad turn to chalk up against his family. If he didn't want live out his life as a poor copy of his grandfather, he was going to have to change. Learning humility would be a good place to start. Here Nick caught sight of his grim, cynical face in a shop window. It gave him an unpleasant shock. If that was how he'd looked earlier, no wonder Catherine had resisted his advances

Catherine.

That was the nub of it. He wanted her. And he couldn't have her. There were no promises he could make to her that he wouldn't break, and she was too decent to be taken with anything less than honesty.

As his thoughts revolved, he realised that what he was staring at through the glass was a crowded furniture emporium. A glance above the door confirmed the name. 'Let's see if we can get at least one thing right today, shall we?' he muttered.

A little later he headed across the road towards the livery yard behind Bottom's coaching office, vowing to be more open-minded and adaptable. Adam and

Catherine had both done it. He could too. Meanwhile, he needed to be astride Satan where he was in control.

★ ★ ★

The bustle of Newmarket Heath, the familiar noise and confusion of horses and curricles, all combined to restore Nick to himself. This was better. This was his milieu. He put ten guineas on Canvas to win the first sweepstake and wheeled around to see who else was here. Everyone, it seemed. He exchanged greetings with a couple of acquaintances, returned a civil nod to a crony of his grandfather who gave him an affronted look, and then made for the Rowley Mile starting post which also marked the beginning of the Two Year Old Course.

'So, you're here then?'

Nick called on centuries of his despised breeding as Viscount Perivale, together with Messrs Chesterfield and Richards trotted up to him, their faces alight at the thought of roasting him some more.

'Where else would I be?' he said in a languid tone. 'It seems eccentric to drive sixty miles to the final Newmarket meeting of the year and then not attend it.'

'Thought you might be tucked up with your ladybird.' Perry guffawed as if he'd said something amusing.

'You will have your little joke. Did you have a wager on my not being present? I do apologise. I hope you haven't dropped too much.'

'A pony. No matter. Didn't think you'd really miss, but there's always that chance, eh?'

'Not where horses are concerned. Who've you got in this one?'

'Slender Billy.'

Nick shook his head in sorrow. 'You are going to have to give up on these lost causes, Perivale. I grant you he was good in his day, but there are younger cattle around now.'

He galloped alongside the others as they followed the race, but peeled away before seeing Canvas come home comfortably in the lead. Instead he headed up to the Running Gap where the start of the next race was to take place.

'Dacre! Ho, Dacre!'

Nick affected not to hear the shout behind him and picked up speed, realising too late that he was heading for a group of gentlemen of no common importance.

'Good day, your Grace,' he said as one of these august personages turned enquiringly at his approach. 'My grandfather charged me to pass on his compliments, should I run across you.'

'The devil he did,' remarked the Duke of Rutland. 'This was before your latest escapade, I take it?'

Nick winced. 'You've heard of that, have you?'

'Such a choice morsel, you cannot be surprised at its being known. Viscount Perivale was full of it.' The rest of the group looked amused in a well-bred fashion.

'If Viscount Perivale would only keep his hands free of other people's private carriages no one need have been aware of it at all,' said Nick. 'Hauled the door open at Hatfield, bold as you please. Bosky, naturally.'

Now there was a rumble of disapproval. 'That man is a positive menace,' said the Duke. 'After he'd finished laughing at you, he had the infernal cheek to ask if I knew all of the landowners around here! Bad blood in the family, of course. I sent him off with a flea in his ear.'

'Looking to marry a local heiress, perhaps,' said Nick. 'He's deep dipped, so I hear.'

'My dear boy, I neither know nor care. How is that enchanting mother of yours, *la belle Héloise*?'

Enchanting. That was how they all saw her. The most carefully contrived piece of fiction in Society. 'She is amusing herself in London by preparing a birthday ball for my grandfather. I have no doubt you will all receive cards.'

'I look forward to it.'

'That makes one of us, my lord.'

The duke looked amused. 'Come and dine at Cheveley tonight. I don't ask you to bring your lady friend.'

'I could not in any case, sir. She neglected to furnish me with her name or direction.' Nick hesitated. 'I am fully sensible of your kindness in extending the invitation, but I believe in view of that very incident, I must decline. It is a little too soon, I fear. I would not put her Grace to the blush.'

'Wednesday, then.' The older man looked at him keenly. 'Not all you seem, are you, young Dacre?'

Nick managed to look scandalised. 'I beg you will not favour my grandfather with your opinion. I have put a great deal of effort into his disapproval of me.'

There was general laughter at this. Nick took the opportunity to change the subject. 'Do you have horses running today?'

'Not today, no. Rhoda has been entered in the handicap sweepstakes tomorrow.'

'Then I wish you the best of luck. Good day, sir. Good day, gentlemen.' He inclined his head gracefully to the company and eased Satan into a trot at a slight angle to their trajectory. He supposed he should now do the filial thing and drop a note to his mother indicating that an invitation to the Duke and Duchess of Rutland would produce a favourable result. It might deflect at least a handful of the coals from his head when he returned home next week.

He became aware of a brown gelding drawing up next to him. 'You are looking pensive, Dacre,' said an amused voice. 'Is the entertainment not riveting enough for you?'

Nick gave a start, masking it with a pull on the reins causing Satan to jib sideways. Alex Rothwell, by all that was great and good! The perfect person to solve his conundrum.

'Good day, Rothwell. I never find the two-horse races as exciting, though my expression just now is down to contemplating the disaster that will shortly be my grandfather's birthday ball. I seem to have inadvertently invited the Duke and Duchess of Rutland to it, meaning I cannot cry off.'

'You'd not be able to anyway,' pointed out Lord Rothwell with discouraging accuracy. He scrutinised the pair of runners for the next race jockeying for position at the starting post. 'Gazelle has the better lines, but Ranksborough is faster over a mile, wouldn't you say? I had a note this morning from Fitz. Anything I can help with?'

Both of them were conversing with the polite half-attention common to members of the same set. No one, thought Nick, would know them for the colleagues and close friends they really were. He kept his eyes on the starter, now raising his handkerchief in the air. 'Indeed you can if you know John Bowman. We are all of us mightily interested in whether anyone has been enquiring about his long-lost sister.'

'Nothing easier,' replied his companion. 'I saw him by the finishing post in the Furzes with a tediously loud country set. Do you care to accompany me down there and watch my brother-in-law's horse romp home to victory in the next?'

'Might as well,' said Nick in the same indifferent tone. 'Nothing more will be happening up here for a while.'

John Bowman, when they discovered him, was in high fettle, having backed the winners of the previous two races. So had Nick, but he wasn't shouting it about. There might be a surer way of getting his pocket picked when he collected his winnings tomorrow morning in town, but he wouldn't take bets on it. Alex greeted Bowman in a distant affable way, congratulated him on his perspicacity and enquired in a polite fashion after his sister.

'She's in London with my stepmother,' said Bowman, scowling. 'Damned if I know why she's so popular today. You're the second person who's been asking. They're staying with her godmother. Both of them spending beyond their means, I don't doubt. Got some madcap scheme about swapping the dower house for a financial consideration and never bothering me again. I'm very tempted, I tell you.'

London? Godmother? Nick was baffled until he realised Bowman was referring to Verity, not Catherine.

Alex Rothwell was forwarder than him. 'That would be why my wife hasn't seen her lately,' he said smoothly. 'I believe she had an excursion in mind. No doubt your other enquirer had a similar idea.'

'What's that? No, never seen the fellow in my life. Damned impertinence I call it.'

And never a question as to who he was or why he wanted to know. And not even a thought as to *which* sister. Bowman and his father alike had simply cut Catherine from the family. Nick fixed his gaze on the course, disgusted.

6

Nicholas was hating this, thought Kitty as she hurried back down to the laundry having seen him safely away. She couldn't blame him. He might make it a point of pride not to bring a valet with him, but always before he would have had inn servants to take the man's place. He was as lost without anyone to keep the fabric of his daily life washed, pressed and brushed as she had been herself when Simon first brought her to London. The difference between them was that she had had no option but to learn. Different worlds, that was the crux of the matter.

'He's gone to the course,' she reported to Adam, and then laughed to see her daughter rubbing the inside of the windows with a rag, mirroring the movements Adam was making as he washed the outside.

'Never fails to amuse,' said Adam with a grin. 'Once you're settled, you must bring her over to Rooke Hall to meet my Lottie. Children need friends.'

Once they were settled. At the moment that felt a lot more like a dream than a promise.

Adam continued. 'Jenny will be glad to see you too. I daresay you used to know her, didn't you? You'd be about the same age and people always know each other in the country. It was one of the things I forgot when I was travelling around. The outside world grew larger, but my inner one shrank until the Chartwell Players became my whole life. It's been odd, growing roots again, but you find you never really forget.'

No, you don't forget, however much you want to. Kitty stacked Molly some firewood by way of finishing up and they were walking back to the house when a horse pulling a cart piled high with an assortment of furniture turned in between the gateposts.

'Furniture already?' she said. 'Goodness, I hope Nicholas didn't bribe him too much.'

'Mrs Redding?' called the carter. 'Gentleman said you needed these as a matter of urgency.'

'Beds for the cottage!' said Kitty as she got closer. 'God bless the man.'

Adam gave the carter a hand unloading. Also on the wagon were a table and chairs for the cottage, a serviceable dresser and a small pretty chest and night-stand painted with wreaths of roses. Kitty assumed these last were for another customer.

'There's a note with these pieces,' said the carter. 'For Miss Ann Redding, with Mr Dacre's compliments. That you, missy?'

Ann nodded, speechless.

Oh, Nicholas. Kitty felt her heart thump. A peace offering. 'They are very pretty,' said Kitty. 'That is so kind of him.'

Ann was desperate to see her new riches safely stowed, so Adam good-naturedly carried them up to her room before they moved the rest to the cottage.

'And now I'm off to saunter about the High Street,' he said once they were done. 'A man with valises never occasions comment, especially during a racing week. I'll direct your Molly here, then get away home. Have you got the letter to Verity you want me to send? Jenny can enclose it in a note from her. They'll be fixed in town for a while yet.' He paused, looking at her carefully. 'You'll be all right?'

'I'll be busy enough. There's a stew to make for tonight, bedding to look for and I won't open the door to anyone except Molly and her mother. I'll set Ann to keep watch for them through the window. Thank you so much for all your help. Do please pass on my good wishes to Jenny. Tell her . . . tell her I would very much like to see her again.'

With Adam gone, the house felt larger than ever. Kitty occupied herself with meat and onions, sent Ann and the cat off to explore for useful closets and chests and thought she had herself under control.

And then her gaze fell on the chair Nicholas had sat in and she was undone again in an instant.

She was being foolish. This instant attraction meant nothing. Hadn't she learnt anything from her wayward past? Nicholas was quality and dangerous. Also a libertine, she added, as her subconscious did not seem convinced, though she was hardly in a position to pass judgement there. They lived in different spheres, that was the circumstance to concentrate on. She should be content with the safety and anonymity she had found. And she was, truly, except for the feeling of constantly having to look over her shoulder.

'Ann,' she called. 'Where are you? We want to be ready for when Molly and the girls arrive.'

Ann was in one of the back bedrooms, hauling slithery satin coverlets out of a chest, much to the joy of the cat. Kitty felt a swell of love to see her so happy. Glancing through the window, the view showed the heath stretching off into the distance, crowded, presumably, with all the race-going gentlemen for miles around. She thought of Kennet End, just four miles away in the other direction. Four miles was nothing. The route around the fields and through the lanes had come back to her the moment she'd set eyes on Newmarket again.

It seemed such a waste, her brother John at the races, his study unguarded and her with a letter in her basket to be delivered there. She straightened her shoulders. She had promised Nicholas she wouldn't go anywhere today. She hadn't mentioned anything about tomorrow.

★   ★   ★

Molly Turner arrived in a long stream of chatter, too voluble at first to even be awed at the size of the house Kitty was leading her past.

'You could've knocked us down with a feather when your man-mountain hands us out of the stage like gentry and asks if we was for Mrs Catherine

Redding at Furze House. And I'm just about to say no, when he tips me the wink and I guessed he meant you. Prudent that is, changing your name. Is this where we are? Well, look at that, Ma, nice size rooms I must say and our own front door. Me and the kiddies upstairs and the room behind this one for you to save your poor legs. Will this be the wash house? Lord, we'll never fill half of it. Oh, I like these long sinks, don't you? And the pump handy in the yard. What a place, eh? I daresay we'll get used to the quiet, but no other buildings behind gives me goose-skin, that's for sure.'

She stopped to draw breath. Looked around the laundry. Looked across at the gardener's cottage with the hens pecking outside the door and the neat rows of vegetables beyond. Frowned. 'Where are you then, Kitty?'

Kitty indicated the main house.

Molly's mouth fell open. 'Never say so!'

'Verity is marrying Charles Congreve. My stepmother is to wed also. Neither of them will be here all the time, so I'm to be housekeeper and lodgings mistress. Molly, it is wonderful that you are in Newmarket, but how do you come to arrive so soon? I did not expect to see you this sennight at least.'

Molly and her mother exchanged glances. Old Ma Turner shrugged. 'You'll have to tell her, Moll.'

'Tell me what?'

Molly checked that the girls were happily climbing up and down stairs and out of earshot. 'Saturday, the streets were busy. I went out to find a bit of work, but what I heard made me come home without. Ma was right surprised. 'That you, Moll? You're early,' she says and I ask who else would it be and tell her Sim Eastwick's been killed, and that he was knifed right there in the street when Mr Congreve was taking him in charge for cheating and procuring. We both knew who must be behind it. Got to be. Afraid Sim would talk.'

'So I think too,' said Kitty soberly.

'I went straight to Henrietta Street to

find you, but you'd gone and the rooms were already looted.'

'I heard. No time wasted there.'

'Yes, but listen. I spoke to the landlady's boy and he said two quiet gentlemen let themselves in ahead of everyone else. Ghost men he called them. They went through everything, *everything*, and left the door ajar when they left.'

Two quiet gentlemen. Horror crept along Kitty's veins. She couldn't move. The icy memory she had tried to lock beyond reach washed over her.

Molly was still talking. 'So I told young Billy to shut his mouth tight, then I went on to the theatres and found Fred Grimes. He's sweet on your Verity. He'd know what was going on if anyone did.'

'Sweet on you, more like,' put in her mother, pulling out a chair and lowering herself on to it.

Molly made a hushing motion. 'He told me you were being hurried to Newmarket. We all knew the next thing would be people looking for information from your friends, so we decided to up sticks as soon as may be.'

Ma Turner nodded slowly. 'Likes everything tidy, that man.'

Tidy. The hood. Cold, dispassionate instructions.

'Mr Congreve give Fred money for the stage for us. Real thoughtful I call that. We told folk we were off to see Lizzie in Peckham. I ran down to the Golden Cross fast as I could and bought tickets. Mr Congreve said to book all the way to Norwich, then get off early to throw anyone off the trail. Shocking waste.'

'Better to waste coin than lives, Moll,' said her mother.

Two quiet men. Kitty hoped her pallor would be taken as agreement. 'Adam said Fred Grimes was bringing your effects?'

Molly nodded. 'Fred'll pick up our bundles from the carrier's office and bring 'em up easy in the cab. He's not been happy since his missus died.

Dicky's coming with him. He's bright enough and sharp. Fred'll be glad of him. And it was one less for the stage.'

Kitty rubbed her brow. 'There are rooms by the stable he can have, but I haven't so much as looked at them yet.'

'That'll not take a trice now we're here.'

Ann tumbled back into the room with Peg and Nell. 'Can I show them the house, Mama? Can I show them all the things?'

'We'll all go,' said Kitty. 'There's a stew cooking and a loaf of bread and a plum pudding, and the kitchen is warmer than it is here.'

'Ann's happy,' observed Molly as Kitty let them in through the side door.

'Thankfully. I didn't think she'd get used to the difference so soon, but she has.'

'And you?'

Kitty shook her head. 'I'm adrift, Molly. Furze House is too big. I daresay I will become accustomed — especially once Verity is here turning everything upside down with her schemes — but at present I am clinging to my two rooms and the kitchen like a drowning man with a raft.' She swallowed. 'And I'm scared.'

'That'll be it, more than the rest,' said Molly. 'Are you in here by yourself then?'

'Charles Congreve's friend Mr Dacre is here too. He is here for the racing, but has been helping us settle in. Adam Prettyman stayed last night. I knew his wife a thousand years ago. It will be strange meeting her again. Readjusting is very hard.'

'That's not surprising, when you think of it. You've changed since we first knew you.'

Kitty smiled briefly. 'I've grown up. This — coming back — would be easier without the fear, Molly.'

Her friend nodded. 'For us too. This Mr Dacre, is he one of them? Like Mr Congreve?'

'Yes. It was him who brought us up here. They call themselves the Pool, but you are not to tell anyone else that. He says he bought you supper once, trying to find out about Flint.'

'Oh, he's that one. Lovely manners. Proper gentleman. I thought he was one of the lonely ones at first, when all he wanted was a bit of company over supper. A lot of them just want to talk. But then I saw the way he was directing the conversation so I said my thank you and left. Best thing to do, no matter how nice they seem. I might say a bit more now though if you and Mr Congreve are vouching for him, not that there's much.' She looked speculatively sideways. 'Lovely looking, isn't he?'

Kitty refused to be drawn. 'Very.'

Molly chuckled. 'Don't fret, I'm not one to poach. Good number of gentlemen and hotels in the town, I must say, from what we saw walking up.'

'The inns are there all year round, but the gentlemen will largely be gone by the end of the week. They're here for the racing and this is the last meeting until April.'

Molly exchanged a glance with her

mother. 'Is that so?'

Kitty felt a twinge of unease. 'Molly, Furze House is to be a respectable establishment. I've promised.'

'And so it will be,' said Molly, patting her arm. 'You know me. No custom through the door unless it's mending or laundry.'

After eating, the others went back to make the laundry cottage their own. Kitty closed the door behind them with regret. She put Ann to bed, took candles into the sitting room, picked up a gown of her mother's she was altering to fit herself and bent her head to her sewing while she waited for Nicholas.

'You look very comfortable,' he said when he came in. He sounded tired and strained. 'I hope you were not waiting up for me. I took you at your word and have spent time with what feels like my whole acquaintance today. The only untoward circumstance I've discovered is that somebody *has* been asking your brother about his sister. He assumed they meant Verity and told them she was in London. That made me so cross that it was a good thing he was talking to Alex Rothwell, not me. Why are you sitting alone? I pictured you with people around you. Did your friends not arrive?'

'Yes, Adam directed them here and then he went home. We ate together. Ann loved having Peg and Nell to inn around with. But it had been a long day for them so they went back early.' She re-threaded her needle. 'Molly was delighted with the size of the laundry cottage.'

'As you said she would be. You are allowed one smug boast.'

She chuckled. 'Oh, and I must thank you for Ann's furniture. She was transported. You are now her favourite person in the world, even more so than Adam.'

'I am glad they found favour. It was to make amends for my less than amiable temper this morning.'

'There was no need. It was a lovely thing to do. She has so little of her own.'

'No, you could not bring much.'

She gave him a frank look. 'There was not much to bring. Anything of value that came into the house, Simon either pawned or sold. A gambler has no sense of right or wrong. Everything is currency.' She took a quick breath. 'In your own words on the way here, I am unlikely to run out of nightmares.'

'They will fade.'

'I do not think so. Not these. It is wonderful having Molly's family here, but it has brought my two lives together again. It has shown me that the past cannot be simply run away from.'

He dropped into the chair opposite, his dark eyes resting on her with disquieting perspicacity. 'You mean, I take it, that things once done are always with us.' There was a bitter note in his voice.

'Very much so.' One day she might have to tell him some of those things. Now, however, there was something of rather more importance. Kitty moistened her lips. 'Molly said the apartment in Henrietta Street had been ransacked.'

'Adam had already mentioned that.'

'Yes, but Molly spoke to my landlady's son. Two quiet gentlemen went there *before* the looters arrived. Ghost men, he called them. They scared him.'

Nicholas grew alert. 'Ghost men? From Flint? Would he recognise them again? The more of Flint's thugs we know, the better able we will be to get a line on him.'

'By now, Billy's mother will have told him he saw nothing. Nicholas, I have been thinking. Those men would not have known what they were looking for.'

'No, but they didn't find it because you told me the information — such as it was — was hidden in your cookery book which you brought with you.'

'That is not what I meant. They did not know what Simon might have left, or in what form. They could have had instructions to bring back any piece of writing, but would Flint have trusted them not to read it, to find out what Simon knew and thus have a hold on

150

him themselves?'

He frowned. 'What are you saying?'

Kitty screwed up her courage and squeezed the words out. 'It is in my mind that one of those quiet gentlemen must have been Flint. Who could he depend on, absolutely and completely, but himself?'

Nicholas stared at her for a full five seconds before looking at his pocket watch and springing for the table to pull pen and paper towards him. 'I must write to Fitz. The mail goes at half past eleven. That's twenty minutes. If Charles can get hold of the lad . . . if he can get any sort of description . . . '

'He can try, but let him approach Billy very, very carefully please. The boy had much better be blind, deaf and dumb now. Or else he will find he really is.'

'I'll tell him. Fitz can take him into service on one of his country estates. That will keep him out of harm's way.' Nicholas wrote rapidly, blew on the ink to dry it, sealed the sheet, wrote the address and hurried out.

Agitation fluttered through Kitty's veins. It had been such a long, strange day, yet she knew she would get little sleep. The two quiet gentlemen were in her head, awaiting their moment. The nightmares were lurking.

Nicholas was back before she'd finished putting away her sewing. 'I cannot see to set another stitch,' she said. She glanced around, checking all was tidy. 'Shall I leave the candles for you?'

'No, I'll come up. What do you have for me to do tomorrow? It's a short race day, so there will be plenty of time.'

'Is it?' she said, disconcerted. 'Does that mean John will not be on the heath? I thought to walk to Kennet End to deliver Mama's letter to Cook and then, if all seemed quiet, reconnoitre my old home.'

Nicholas's brows drew together. 'Can the dower house be seen from the main dwelling? In view of your brother's disclosures today, I cannot think it wise to reacquaint him with a sister he has clearly expunged from memory.'

'You said you were cross with him for that!'

He looked shamefaced. 'I was cross with everything. Principally with myself for not being able to adapt.'

'You have not been brought up to.'

'Nor were you.'

'I have had seven years to accustom myself. You have had two days. You appear to be making good progress to me. Do you not see, Nicholas? I had little choice, especially once I had Ann to care for. And also, for most of those seven years I thought it was my own fault so there was no barrier in my head telling me I should not need to do any of it.'

'As there is in mine, you mean? I am clearly more transparent than I thought.'

The words were bitter. He was blaming himself for his own upbringing. Kitty turned the conversation. 'Tell me again what John said?'

'Only that his sister was in London.

Fortunately Alex Rothwell caught his drift before I did and diverted him with some remark about an excursion. Do you know Rothwell? His brother-in-law runs a training yard in the town. Harry Fortune. Though I believe it is Caroline who trains the more contrary animals.'

Kitty's jaw dropped. 'Caroline? Your friend is married to Caroline Fortune? But . . . ' She paused. 'I was going to say he could not be, for she was quite a little girl when I left. But then, so was Verity.' She looked at him ruefully. 'Again I find I am caught between two worlds. It keeps happening. Adam said I must bring Ann to visit his wife, who was Jenny Rooke when I knew her, but I am afraid to for fear she will no longer know me. Everyone here has moved on. I don't fit any more.'

'You will,' said Nicholas with conviction. 'You will readapt.'

'Not if I am to be watchful every time I leave the house. It is hard to be sociable if one is never to relax.'

He crossed the room and took her

shoulders. 'Then we will track down Flint and deliver him to justice, either by searching your father's study for a clue to the past or by discovering Flint's agent here and getting a name out of him.'

He was so very confident, so very sure. For a moment she had a deep desire to step closer and rest her head against his chest. She conquered it, but it was an effort. 'Thank you,' she said. 'I apologise for being such a poor creature. It is simply that when I think about what could yet follow me from my other life, I am scared.'

'Scared, yet brave with it.' He let her go and crouched to bank the fire for the night. 'Unlike me. My life is more of a lie than yours. I mix with people of money and rank every day and I have neither. I don't even have my own home. Certainly I have no purpose. While Napoleon was running around Europe I did some translation work for the Admiralty, but they do not need me now, so I am rootless again. And yet I do nothing to change it.'

One of the lonely ones. That was what Molly had said, and he was so good at dissembling that people didn't see there was a wounded core underneath the glamour.

'But you are happy, yes?'

His mouth twisted. 'Most of the time I am what passes for happy.'

The atmosphere between them had changed. Kitty spoke slowly. 'All I wish for is safety for Ann, a few good friends, the nightmares to stay away, and a small country life that I can truly call my own. What would you choose if you could?'

'Hah.' Nicholas gave a short laugh. 'I have never dared to think. Horses. Time. Time of my own. A competence that is mine by right, or that I have earned myself. Freedom.'

'Freedom would be something indeed.' She lit two candles from the branch on the table, handed one to him and pinched out the originals.

'You do not ask why.' His face was shadowed in the dim glow of the fire.

'We all have our demons.' She started to walk up the stairs.

He followed her. 'As I said before, you are an unusual woman.'

One of the lonely ones. And too proud to ask. And her with nightmares waiting.

She filled her lungs resolutely. This would be a risk. Dared she take it? Did she trust him? 'Do you . . . do you ever feel the need simply for comfort?' she asked.

Behind her, she heard an indrawn breath.

'No contracts,' she said, keeping her gaze on the circle of candlelight lighting her path. 'No promises or assumptions. No money changing hands or expectations for the future. Just warmth and sharing and a measure of peace.'

They reached the second landing. She turned, searching his face. 'Just Nicholas and Catherine, together in the darkness.'

He opened his mouth then, his eyes full of pain.

She laid her finger on his parted lips. 'No questions. No commitments. Just comfort.'

He caught her hand, folded it over his own, and kissed it.

7

Nick woke, warm for the first time since arriving in Newmarket, and with his arms wonderfully full of woman. Not just any woman. Catherine. That there had been need on both sides was obvious, but he had not expected so much passion in the quiet darkness.

Things once done. He should have told her then, but the moment had passed with her news of Flint, and then she had made her offer and . . .

She had gone to sleep with her head pillowed in the hollow by his throat. She had moved a little now, so it was an easy matter to free himself. Easy physically, not easy otherwise. She had given unstintingly and reposed complete trust in him. He wanted to prolong this waking moment as far as possible. However, he also had no wish to embarrass her in the light of day, so he kissed her forehead and whispered his thanks before sliding out and seeking his own empty bed for what remained of the dawn. *Always the gentleman, Nicholas.*

★　★　★

Kitty woke alone, but there was a warm impression in the bed next to her and the memory of a kiss on her forehead. The demons had stayed away all night. She tried to find a blush within her for what she had done, but could not. *Just Nicholas and Catherine, together in the darkness.* That's what she'd said and he had taken her at her word. No questions, no commitments, just trust exchanged and a need satisfied. She hadn't felt this safe for years.

Molly came with her when she went out for bread and other supplies, brightly interested in the shops and with an eye for all the places she could advertise their laundry and repairs service. By the time they got back, Ma

Turner had made herself at home in the kitchen and was evidently fast friends with Mrs Green, who was just returning to her cottage with Eliza.

Everyone — including Nicholas — ate breakfast together. Molly greeted him with a cheerful nod. Kitty wished she had half her insouciance.

'Can you look after Ann today?' she asked. 'But don't go out with her and don't open the door to anyone until I'm back. I need to deliver a letter to Mama's cook at Kennet End and fetch some old gowns of Verity's to cut down for Ann.'

'Kennet End?' said Molly. 'Someone mentioned that last night. Wanted to know how to get there.'

There was a pause. Kitty felt her stomach sink. 'Last night? Oh Molly, you didn't go out to find work? Not already?' She didn't dare look at Nicholas.

Her friend gave a matter-of-fact shrug and continued to cut her bacon. 'I'd been cooped up on the stagecoach all day and you told me yourself the gentlemen would only be here a week. Coin is coin. Do you know you have to tip the guard to look after you on the stage? It goes against the grain, I must say, when there were four of us and there's a far cheaper way, but Mr Congreve told us to act like any other travellers going to see family in Norwich, so there you are. Anyway, that's why I needed a bit of work, soon as could be. I gave most of what I had by me to Fred before we left, to help him with bran and stabling for the journey.'

'But . . . ' Kitty resolutely ignored Nicholas's splutter of appreciation from the far end of the table.

'Don't you start arguing. If we're all eating together, we need to put in our bit and there won't be any laundry money until the wash-house is running. Can you write me out some notices for that? You've got better words than me, as well as a better hand. I'll spread them around when I'm going about the town later.'

Nicholas spoke. Kitty thought it had probably taken him this long to get his mirth under control. 'Who was asking about Kennet End? Can you describe him?'

'I didn't see. Right crowded it was. All the gentlemen's clubs in London must be empty. I only remember because of the funny name. End of what?'

'End of Kennet village,' said Kitty. 'It's no funnier than Mile End in London. What else did they say?'

'Someone said it was on the road to Bury and the innkeeper was a thief and a rogue. And someone else said weren't they all and there was a bit of an argy-bargy because the landlord took exception. You can see his point.'

'Which inn was it?' asked Nicholas. 'Which hotel?'

'I'm puzzled to remember now. My gentleman and I slipped out during the fuss. It would have been on this side of the road. I went in two or three. Plenty of 'em, I must say. I'll do a few more tonight.'

'This changes matters,' said Nicholas to Kitty. 'Our man is here for sure. It is not safe for you to go out. I will accompany you to Kennet End.'

'Oh certainly, for that will not occasion comment at all. I daresay gentlemen's carriages are forever calling at the dower house, especially distinctive ones picked out in burgundy and gilt. Nicholas, it is a straight road. The carriage will be visible for miles.'

'You are not walking there alone.'

'Lord above,' cackled Ma Turner. 'You're never telling me men and maids don't go courting in country lanes no more? Your smoky gentleman will bowl past you and never think twice. Run to the pop shop, Moll, and fetch him a slouch and a smock.'

There was a startled silence, then Nicholas burst out laughing. 'Mrs Turner, you are quite splendid. I no longer wonder where your daughter got her talents from.'

★　★　★

164

Nick made one change to the plan, suggesting that he take Catherine up before him on Satan and they ride to the village inn, before he stripped off his concealing greatcoat and they walked the rest of the way. 'It means we can return faster and I can still show my face on the heath,' he explained.

Catherine nodded. 'I'll wait on the corner of the Bury Road. Molly will come with me for cover. Nobody notices two women with their heads together.'

It was a good scheme, but as ill luck would have it, Nick was accosted by Viscount Perivale as he rode past the White Hart.

'Dacre! Where are you off to so early?'

Nick's eyes flicked to the archway of the inn behind him. Perry was dressed for riding and was evidently waiting for his groom to bring out a hack. His usual friends were nowhere in sight. It would never do if he took it into his head to join him.

'Cheveley,' he invented. 'His Grace invited me yesterday. Can't be late. Daresay I'll see you this afternoon.' He went off at a smart lick, reached down a hand to pull Catherine up at the corner and had taken the turn to Bury St Edmunds long before Perry would have been mounted and able to follow.

'Goodness,' said Catherine, balancing against him and breathing only slightly faster than usual. 'One would think oneself at Aspley's Amphitheatre.' She gave an awkward wriggle whilst adjusting her skirts, leading Nick to a distracting recollection of the previous night.

'I apologise for my haste,' he said, trying to sound focused on their journey. 'I didn't think you'd want the company of the gentleman who made free of my carriage at Hatfield.'

He felt her start. 'No indeed,' she said fervently. 'By the by, I have been thinking of our route and have a better idea than going to the inn. Keep on this road for three miles until you see a barn on the left, just past a belt of trees on the right. Stop there. We can conceal Satan in the barn and walk the last mile across the fields.'

'Will the farmer not object?'

Catherine gave a snort of laughter. 'Unless things have changed very much in the last seven years, a couple of pennies in the box by the door ensures no questions will ever be asked. Waterhall Farm borders ours. It was a source of constant aggravation to my father that any number of malefactors could be holed up there, waiting for the chance to raid our sheep or steal our wheat.'

Both the barn and the wooden box were where she had said. Evidently not much had changed at all. They left Satan guarding Nick's hat and greatcoat, and hurried down a narrow track bordering the next field.

'Fertile countryside,' remarked Nick. 'I have never had occasion to examine it this closely before.'

Catherine glanced around. 'It would have been better for us before the harvest was gathered in. More cover.'

For himself, he was glad to be in the open air. She, however, was far more tense than he'd expected. 'Tell me of the household,' he said, both to distract her and because he was curious. 'Will they know you?'

'At the dower house are the cook and the housemaids. Cook will certainly know me, for she has been at Kennet End for ever. Verity says she moved across to the dower house to be with them when my brother and his wife brought in a new French chef. The letter is to invite her to Kensington with Mama. Even if we do not get there before Flint's spy, she would not dream of telling him anything.'

'She will not tell your brother you had visited?'

'No. There is no harm in John, we were good friends when we were children, but as he grew older he spent more and more time with Papa. I am afraid being constantly reminded he was the heir — and being encouraged to act like it — made him pompous and far more inclined to think of his position before considering anyone else. It did not endear him to the servants.'

Two curricles came along the road, the drivers calling cheerfully over the noise of the horses' hooves. Nick caught Catherine's hand and they fell into a slow dawdle, their heads close as if engrossed in each other. 'Last night . . . ' began Nick.

'Was lovely,' she replied quickly. 'Please, no questions. We agreed.'

Her hand was small and firm. It fitted naturally into his. He didn't want to let it go. 'I was only going to say it was lovely for me too. It is rare for me to sleep the night through like that.'

She made a deprecatory motion. 'It had been a long day.'

'It was more than that. There was a sense of affinity and trust. I felt . . . not alone.'

She looked up at him. 'I thought you said your grandfather's house was rarely empty?'

'It is not, but there is no companion-ship there. No affection. No unconditional caring, such as we shared last night. I wanted to thank you.'

'There is no need. I should be thanking you for . . . for behaving like a gentleman.'

For not taking a chance on an unwanted pregnancy. Heat and shame swept through him. His throat filled with burrs. He had done that for him, not her. He had done it for years now. While he was unable to talk, they crossed a lane. The hedges became noticeably better tended. 'Is this your brother's land?' he managed.

'This is Kennet End ground, yes. One more field and we will be at the dower house. My brother's residence is further along.'

She was nervous again. Nick asked no more questions. Instead he enlivened the last stretch with an animadversion on the previous owner of his shirt, whom he seriously doubted had ever washed it.

'Heavens,' he muttered, on seeing the

dower house, 'one can see why your stepmother should prefer a new villa in Kensington.'

'It is truly ugly, is it not? I feel quite grateful I never lived in it. We go around the side here.'

In the yard, she gathered herself, put her shoulders back, then rapped on the door.

'Miss Catherine!' It was plain that the cook recognised her, even after the seven years that had taken her from wilful girl to wary young matron. 'Oh, Miss Catherine, come in with you, do.'

It was the first time Nick had seen tears on Catherine's face. She dashed them away and hugged the woman. 'Yes, it is me and I am very glad to see you again and hope you are well, but we must be quick, for there is a man searching for me and so I must say my piece and be away and if you please, I was never here. This is Mr Dacre who is a friend of Mr Congreve and who is helping me.'

Nick listened, impressed at the economy

with which Catherine imparted her new name and direction, her mother and sister's forthcoming change in circumstances, handed over the letter and finally came to their real purpose.

'Cook, this is very shocking, but we have learnt that before their marriage, my father had the gentleman Mama was betrothed to murdered. I believe there may be a clue to this man in Papa's study. I thought to visit with this note for John and contrive to look around, but Mr Dacre is of the opinion I should not remind them of me in case the man who is searching goes there and asks if I have returned.'

Cook, Nick thought, did not seem entirely surprised at the revelation regarding the late Mr Bowman. 'He's right on that, Miss Catherine, but it's a puzzle to me how you'd look around with Mr John's wife at your heels the whole way, showing off her new decoration scheme.'

Catherine said carefully, 'As to that, I suppose I was principally wondering how much things have changed. I daresay the faulty catch on the study window has been mended by now, for example?'

Cook stared at her, then gave a slow smile. 'Years ago.'

'And is the narrow side-door that was never used still shrouded by a curtain? Does it still have but a single bolt at the base holding it closed?'

'Why yes.' Cook tapped her fingers on the table. 'It would be a shame if you had intended visiting today, for Mr and Mrs Bowman are dining with the Elstridges this evening. Very puffed up about it, Mrs John is. I did think I might step over this afternoon and ask Sarah — she's head housemaid now — if she'd like to join me for a bite of supper. I could take this letter with me, perhaps, and say it was left here by mistake. I daresay I could check that bolt too if you were interested in it.'

'Cook! You'd do that for me?'

'See here, Miss Catherine, I came to Kennet End with your real ma when she married Mr Bowman. He was a cold-hearted man then, and he didn't change.

Your ma was the sweetest creature that ever lived, and your stepma is the kindest. I'll help you for both their sakes.'

Catherine embraced the stout woman and covered her in blushes.

'I'll get a couple of Miss Verity's old gowns and then you'd better be gone. I'll see your daughter one day, I don't doubt.' She eyed Nicholas, sizing up his riding clothes under the country smock. 'You mind my seed cake, Miss Catherine? I'll make one today and leave half of it wrapped up in the stable in case anyone knows of a little girl who might like it. The other half I'll give to the stable boy. He'll be so full he won't stir all night.'

★　★　★

Catherine was quiet when they left, her head downbent. Nick couldn't see her expression under the plain bonnet she wore. 'So, we go back tonight?'

She looked up then. 'You do not need to.'

174

'You must rid yourself of this habit of saying foolish things. Can we take Satan closer to the house than the barn?'

'Yes, that was what Cook was saying. We can use the dower house stable. There is only a boy there, and he will be full of cake. Nicholas, I feel so ashamed. I left without a word seven years ago, yet they are all looking after me and helping me as if I am a favoured daughter.'

Ahead of them, a horse came thundering down the lane, going in the direction of Newmarket. Nick instantly swung Catherine into an embrace, half in half out of the hedge. And just as instantly, he was back in her bed, matching her passion, feeling her warm, vital presence in his arms and in his soul. One glimpse of the rider stayed with him, all brown horse and grey coat and a confusion of puce, blue, tan and green. All else was Catherine.

'Imagine,' she said shakily once the danger had passed and the hoofbeats had died away. 'I used to think alfresco kisses were romantic.'

'Was it not?' asked Nick, his heart thumping and his breathing ragged. He was finding it difficult coming back to himself. He was also finding it difficult letting go of her.

She seemed to be having much the same trouble. 'Nicholas, I . . . ' She stopped, swallowed and stepped away. 'We should get back. I believe you were right about the previous owner of your shirt. I will hang it to air when I return.'

It wasn't until they were in the barn and he'd stuffed the shirt and hat into Catherine's basket that she said in a neutral voice, 'Was that him, do you suppose? Flint's spy?'

'It may have been.' And now he was mortified. From that first touch, she had taken such possession of his mind that he hadn't made any attempt to see more of the rider. He helped her up to Satan's back and felt her tremble. 'I did not see his face. I swear he did not see ours either. It is possible I might recognise him from the general impression, but

176

the only thing I could be sure of was that he rode a brown horse.'

'Oh, well, I'm sure that will be a great help on the heath.'

Nick's short laugh was half appreciation, half anguish. If Fitz could see him now, he'd wonder why he had ever entrusted him with this mission. He needed to get this woman out of his system so he could protect her clear-sightedly.

★   ★   ★

The evening journey was easier, thought Kitty, as much because she didn't have the fear of rejection by Cook ahead of her as because the dusk made it less likely that they'd be recognised. Even so, every footstep brought echoes of the confident, heedless girl she had once been. The wasted years made her want to weep.

They reached the dower house stables, left Satan in a newly swept stall, and walked cautiously through the shrubbery to the main house. Beside Kitty,

Nicholas's step was buoyant. 'Are you enjoying this?' she asked in disbelief.

She heard the laugh in his voice. 'I confess I am. Aren't you?'

'No. It brings back memories of nocturnal escapades when I was younger. I dislike being reminded of poor judgement.'

They flitted around the outside of the grey stone walls until the side door was reached. It was more of a long window, covered on the inside with a thick curtain because it let in a draught. Kitty rested her fingers on the handle, her heart pumping so loudly she thought the whole household must have heard it.

The door opened as easily as ever. *Thank you, Cook.*

'Which way when we are inside?' asked Nicholas in a low voice.

She shook her head. 'I'll not have you charged with housebreaking. You are in trouble enough with your grandfather through me. Stay here. No one will see you in the embrasure.'

'I cannot let you do this alone.'

'This was my secret way in and out of the house for years. I will be there and back within ten minutes.'

'And if you are not?'

'Then ride for home as fast as you can. No one will connect you with me.'

His clasp on her arm was steady. 'I repeat, which way when we are inside? I give you my word I will not move unless I have to.'

She met his implacable gaze, knowing he would not leave without her. It gave her a ridiculously warm feeling, but increased the pressure on her to be successful. 'Down the passage and it is the second door on the right. But I will be back.'

He nodded and let her go.

The house was quiet. Kitty moved quietly up the freshly-painted passage, skirted an ostentatious side table that her father wouldn't have given house-room to and eased herself into the study. She stood for a moment in the moonlight, getting her bearings, but there was no need. Whatever changes her brother's wife had wrought in the rest of the house, this room had not altered at all. Her father's character was still stamped on it. She beat back an unexpected swell of rage at the memory of him, crossed to the desk, pulled out the bottom drawer, then felt at the back of the revealed space for the switch.

There was a soft click, and at the same time loud footsteps and voices were heard in the passage. The footmen! Did they still do a check on every room, as they had when her father had been master here? Kitty frantically crammed herself into the recess under the desk and pulled the chair towards her as far as she could, the knuckles of her fingers white where she gripped the carved legs. The footsteps paused, the study door was opened and closed, the footsteps went on.

Kitty breathed again. Easing herself slightly, she opened the newly released panel in front of her and peered inside.

There was just enough moonlight coming through the window to see a significant film of dust coating everything in the hidden compartment. A wave of thankfulness passed through her. John did not know the desk's secret. She wasted no more time, but swept all the contents into the drawstring bag she had ready. Then she closed the panel, wriggled out, put chair and drawer back and trod softly to the study door, breathing fast and listening for sounds from outside.

From the front hall she heard the two footmen gossiping in a way they wouldn't if John was home. Good. If they were talking, they wouldn't be attending any too carefully to a rattle of rings or a betraying gust of air from the side door. She made her way swiftly down the passage. As she reached the heavy curtain she saw it move. Heart in mouth she readied her fist and then tweaked the edge of the curtain with her other hand.

'Twelve minutes,' breathed Nicholas

in her ear. 'But I forgive you. Did you get it?'

'I got everything. I have no idea what it all is until we get home.'

'Come then. Let's go.'

8

What had been hidden behind the panel? The ride back passed in a blur as that one question beat insistently in Kitty's head. She could feel the bag pressing against her ribs, covered and secured there by her cloak doubled around her body. There was something large and soft, that she did know. There was also something lumpy that dug in, something heavy that dragged it down, something with corners . . .

They slowed as they reached Newmarket. Nicholas took Satan right, towards the church, and up around the backs of the houses to avoid the main road. There were far too many gentlemen strolling along the High Street in search of food, entertainment and diversion for it to be safe to go the direct route. Kitty slid down Satan's flank at the back gate and hurried up past the stable block and through the yard. Nicholas continued onwards towards the heath in order to arrive presently at the livery stable from the opposite direction.

Mrs Green's hens set up a sleepy squawk as she passed the hen house. 'Hush, you silly creatures, it's only me,' she said, and sped on until she reached the side door. In the kitchen, the feeling of normality almost overset her. Ma Turner and the girls were at the table hemming handkerchiefs out of the scraps of linen Ann had found, Molly was putting on her bonnet ready to go out.

'Any trouble?' asked Molly.

'None,' replied Kitty. 'Though I cannot think I am cut out for a housebreaker's life.'

Her friend nodded comfortably. 'I'll be off then. I'll see you later, Ma.'

Kitty swung the kettle on to boil. She had begun to shake and needed the comfort of a pot of tea. How long would Nicholas be? If he met any of his friends after stabling Satan, he might go with them to one of the hotels.

'You want to sit down before you fall down,' observed Ma Turner shrewdly.

'I do.' Kitty sat with them and drank her tea and for five minutes filled her head with nothing beyond praising the neatness of the girls' stitches, speculating on when Fred Grimes might get here and talking over what else might be needed for the laundry.

Ma Turner took Nell and Peg home, and Kitty put Ann to bed. She had just taken the drawstring bag through to the sitting room when the front door opened and Nicholas walked in.

'My apologies,' he said, 'I ran into some acquaintances and thought it best to be my normal convivial self. Well? What have you found?'

'I haven't looked,' she confessed. 'Everyone was here and I ... I suddenly couldn't do anything but sit.'

He nodded, understanding. 'I am the same after a fierce fencing bout. All the extra energy extracts a price. You are recovered now?'

'Yes. Thank you. Shall we look? I am glad you were no later. I wanted you with me when I opened the bag. I felt you had the right.'

Pleasure lit his face. 'Let us get to it then.'

The large, soft item proved to be an embroidered silk shawl in a silk bag. 'Why would this be hidden?' said Kitty wonderingly, and tipped the rest of the contents on top of it.

Nicholas pounced on a small, well-filled notebook. 'This could be what we want. Curse the man for writing in such a cramped hand. I need better light to make any of the words out. Have we more candles? Wait, what is this near the beginning? *Mrs Hennessy has given me a name.* Who is Mrs Hennessy?'

Kitty shook her head. 'No one I know.' She reached for a blue velvet pouch and drew out a delicate silver locket. The silver was tarnished, but Kitty recognised it straight away. Her anger against her father nearly choked her.

'This is Mama's locket,' she said. 'She was wearing it the first time I met her. I was younger than Ann is now, but when she saw me looking, she took it off straight away and let me hold it. I asked about it some years later and she said she'd lost it. He must have hidden it from her. What a wicked, petty thing to do. I am glad I hated him.' A tear fell on the delicate filigree decoration. Kitty rubbed it dry, then felt for the catch at the side. The locket sprang open.

Nicholas leant across to see, his breath caressing her cheek. 'Who is that?' he asked. 'Your father?'

Kitty looked at the young, smiling face in the painted miniature. 'No, this is a much more personable man. I think it must be Will Lawrence, the man Papa paid to have killed. He was Verity's real father, though nobody but Mama knew that. That's why she had to get married so fast.' She lifted her face to Nicholas. 'I will clean the locket and return it to her. I wonder if the shawl is hers too? It is very fine, though I do not think deep red is a colour she would wear. Maybe that is why it seems so new. Perhaps Will Lawrence gave it to her and Papa was jealous. Taking it from her would be a punishment. He was not a likeable man.'

'He sounds worse than my family, if such a thing were possible. What are the other items? What is the folded sheet of paper?'

The writing was in a hand Kitty knew well. She could barely bring herself to smooth the folds. 'It is from Simon,' she said, her voice flattening. 'It says he agrees to elope with me and marry me for the sum of a thousand pounds, five hundred to be paid on this signature, five hundred on delivery of proof to Messrs D&D, London. They are Papa's attorneys.' She stood abruptly, tears threatening to flow again.

'Catherine . . .' Nicholas's arms came around her. 'Hush. Give the paper to me and I will send it to Charles to keep with the other documents they found. You do not need to see it again.'

'I am sorry. In time I may no longer

feel like a gaming chip.' She clung to him for a moment, feeling the strong, lean safety of his body, then gave a mighty sniff and turned back to the table. 'Oh!' Pushing Simon's agreement across to him, she gave a sudden glad smile and reached for a small box. She knew what this was but had hardly dared find it here. Her movements dislodged an unevenly-shaped pebble. As it rolled across the table, her whole body stilled.

Nicholas picked the pebble up. 'What's this? Ammunition for a sling? Did he confiscate it from your brother for breaking a window, perhaps?'

Kitty felt herself drain of colour. The box fell from her hand. What he held was a rounded, misshapen white stone with darker patches showing through the stone's hollows. 'It is not for a sling,' she said, forcing the words out. 'Even if it was, it would be me that used it, not John. I always had by far the better eye.'

Nicholas squinted at it, turning it

over in his hand. 'What then?'

She moistened her lips. 'I am guessing your grandfather's estate is not in this part of the country.'

He looked even more mystified. 'No, it is in Yorkshire. My eldest uncle lives there with my cousins and their ever-increasing families. He manages it for a pittance, in the faint hopes that it will one day be his to pass on. Why?'

'Because this kind of stone, as both large lumps and small pebbles, is found across Suffolk, and I think Norfolk too. It is turned over in fields by the harrow, and used for building our walls and churches. When cut and dressed it is used for making handsome patterns on the face of grand buildings.'

'This piece of stone?' he said sceptically. 'It does not look that impressive.'

'It is only chalky white on the outside. Within, it is coal black. The cut edge strikes a spark to make fire. It is flint, Nicholas. This is a nodule of flint.'

'Flint?' He let out a long whistle. 'A

calling card, you think?'

She met his eyes, feeling sick to her very soul. 'Or a receipt.'

There was a roaring in her ears. Memories threatened to overwhelm her. Now she knew for sure, when before it had been only conjecture. Because four years ago, when the hood had been removed and she'd stumbled half-senseless out of the cab, she had found a dressed flint in the pocket of her cloak. For days afterwards she had no idea how it had got there. She had left it on the dresser where Ann should not pick it up and cut herself. She hadn't noticed when it had disappeared. Now she realised the flint had not been hers at all. It had been for Simon.

★　★　★

Catherine had turned the colour of parchment. Nick caught her when she swayed and would have fallen. 'What is the matter?' he said, alarmed. He helped her to the sofa. 'Have you eaten since you got back? Shall I fetch some wine?'

'I have drunk tea,' she said. She was shivering as if she couldn't control herself. 'Please . . . please just hold me.'

'That is easy. It is something I have been wanting to do all day.' He pulled her on to his lap and cradled her against him. She was as insubstantial as a leaf.

'I am so sick of this, Nicholas.' Her voice was muffled by his chest. 'I am so sick of not being able to live my life. Will everything I have done over the past seven years continue to haunt me forever?'

He held her close and pressed his lips to her forehead. 'We will expunge it. There will be a cleansing and a burning. I swear it.'

She gave a shaky laugh. 'When you say it so fiercely, I can almost believe you. I do not think it is possible.'

Her hair was soft against his cheek. 'If we don't, it will not be for the want of trying. I very much wish to know what has upset you, but you do not have to tell me anything — unless it will help us catch the spy faster.'

'This has nothing to do with the spy. It does have to do with Flint, though it will not help you locate him. And yes, I will tell you, but not yet. I do not quite know how.'

'Whenever you are ready then.'

'Just like that?'

'In your own words, Catherine, we all have our demons.'

She lay against him a little longer. He felt her shivers die down and guarded himself against the moment she moved away. 'We should look at the notebook,' she said eventually, and then, 'Will you stay with me tonight?'

A tremor, or possibly a thunderbolt, ran through him. 'It will be my privilege. It is also my great desire.'

Another shaky laugh. 'You have beautiful manners, Mr Dacre.'

'All well, that was another thing it was impossible to grow up without in my grandfather's house.'

Beautiful manners, and a burden he could not share. He let her stand with reluctance and they returned to the table.

The initial entries in the notebook were so old the ink had faded. 'Faded and crabbed,' said Nick. 'Are you familiar with your father's hand? Can you read this?'

'I think so.' Catherine held the pages where the light from the candles would illuminate them better. '*Mrs Hennessy established in Northgate Street. Offer made to Miss Murrell. Fifteen thousand pounds.*' She looked at him. 'Murrell was my birth mother's family. Fifteen thousand pounds dowry, and only six settled on me and John between us. That shows you what sort of man my father was.'

'It is a diary then?'

'Partly that, partly accounts. I cannot make out all the dates. John's birth is recorded. Then *Mrs Hennessy agate necklace fourteen guineas, Mrs Hennessy gold ring with cameo five pounds and fifteen shillings . . .* '

194

'I begin to have a glimmering of who Mrs Hennessy might be,' said Nick.

She looked across, round-eyed. 'I too. I am amazed. I would not have thought it at all in character.' She leafed through. 'No mention of my birth, though there is a fine ormolu clock at twelve guineas for Mrs Hennessy at around the right time. Oh!'

She looked suddenly stricken. Nick took the notebook from her and read the entry she had stopped at. *Margaret laid to rest. Miss Harrington is a beautiful girl and has £20,000.*

Disgust filled him. 'Dear God, he wasted no time, did he?'

'Very little,' she said bitterly. 'Did you read the next line?'

Nick looked. In angry capitals that had scored through to the next page were the words *Refused! She will pay for this. I require that £20,000.* His eye travelled down the page to the line he had seen first. *Mrs Hennessy has given me a name.*

He met Catherine's gaze. 'I think we

need to visit Mrs Hennessy. Where is Northgate Street?'

'There is a Northgate Street in Bury St Edmunds. My father used to go to Bury frequently. He said it was on business. And . . . and I did see him go into a house in Northgate Street once. At the time I was principally thankful he had not seen *me* as I was supposed to be at school.'

'Always a rebel,' he teased. 'Would you know the house again?'

'Nicholas, it was years ago. I remember it was towards the abbey ruins, and it had a blue front door . . . '

'Which has almost certainly been painted over by now. There may be more detail in the book. I could wish his writing had been fairer.'

'Shall I look?'

Nick passed it across gladly. He glanced at the table. 'What is in the small box? You didn't open it.'

'I didn't need to.' She smiled and lifted the lid, disclosing a pearl ring in the shape of a flower. 'This one I know.

It is mine and it was my mother's. After she died, my nurse put it on my finger. I wore it for years. Papa wrenched it from my hand during one of our arguments and said I should have it back when I walked down the aisle with a man of his choosing. I was on fire with fury. How strange the way life turns out. I never thought to be grateful to him, but Simon would have sold the ring long since had I been wearing it when we eloped.'

She slipped it on. It was the prettiest piece. The pearls formed the petals of the flower and it was made for a very slender hand. It looked entirely right on her.

'That is lovely,' said Nick. 'I can see why you would have been angry at his taking it. Why did he keep it, do you suppose? He knew you were not coming back.'

Catherine glanced up at him drily. 'I daresay it did not fit Mrs Hennessy's finger.'

He laughed. 'You are wonderful. The rest of this notebook can wait until tomorrow. Shall we retire, Mrs Redding?'

197

'I should like that, Mr Dacre.' She paused. 'Still no commitments.'

He nodded. 'Still no commitments.'

★　★　★

Wednesday. Halfway through his Newmarket week and Nick was no nearer to discovering the identity of Flint's cat's paw. Or was he? That rushed glimpse on the road to Kennet End fretted at his memory. It had included a flash of green.

The house had been silent when he'd awoken for the second time, so he had used the can of hot water considerately placed outside his door to wash and shave and then — mindful of certain home truths told to him the other day — he walked through the yard past the laundry to find everyone sweeping out a loose box and clearing one of the stable cottages.

It stabbed at his pride that Catherine was doing this herself. The lithe, passionate woman who had shared his bed these last two nights should not be ankle-deep in straw and cobwebs. She should be arrayed in silk and fine lawn, in satin and Brussels lace.

And then what? Could she cook a fricassee dressed in satin? Could she lay a fire and boil a kettle decked out in lace?

Nick's fantasy dissolved. She was Catherine, a real person who got on with life, no matter how difficult it was. And he could give her nothing. Nothing except respect. He approached the stable block. The laughter that accompanied their mundane occupation was as baffling as ever. How could anyone find amusement in drudgery? He didn't understand it, but it still caused him a stab of envy.

'I am afraid it will not be possible to go to Bury St Edmunds today,' he said to Catherine. *Lord, but she was beautiful.* 'There is a full racing programme on the heath and I am bidden to Cheveley to dine afterwards.'

'Are you forgiven then?' she asked

with a smile. She had wrapped an apron around her similar to that worn by Molly and Ma Turner and looked entirely wonderful. Was he imagining that she looked at him more warmly than she had yesterday?

Behind her, one of the little girls suddenly leapt up out of a pile of straw, causing the others to shriek and fall about.

Nick grinned. 'I am on the way to it, I believe. The invitation was by way of a command. For some reason beyond my comprehension, the Duke of Rutland appears determined to reinstate me in society after our misadventure on the road.'

'I will see you later then. I will go through the notebook to see if there are any more clues.'

'That would be useful.' He cleared his throat. 'I . . . I may be late.'

Her eyes danced, answering the question he dared not ask in front of Molly and her mother. 'It matters not,' she said, and then went on as if it was part of the same sentence. 'I will leave the door unbarred. You have the key. What do you think, Nicholas? This box will do for Fred Grimes's horse if he arrives today, won't it? The straw was here already and Mr Green has very kindly arranged some hay.'

Nick surveyed the stall with a covetous eye. 'It will do very well. I was thinking, once this business is settled, I would like to have the convenience of stabling Satan here. The carriage horses too. Another project to put in hand. As it is, I shall go and take breakfast in the White Hart and see if my coachman has picked up any choice morsels from his confederates regarding doings in London.'

He left before he said any more. It was not just his horses he would like the convenience of stabling here. He was starting to want the right to stay here openly himself. And that was impossible.

In the White Hart dining room, he chose a table near the door, falling easily into conversation with the gentle-men already seated at it. Thus when Viscount Perivale strolled in, holding forth to Chesterfield on the subject of today's runners, he gave the appearance of having been there for some time.

Yesterday Perry had been riding a brown horse. Today he was still wearing the green ribbons. That had to be the low down flash of colour Nick had seen in the Kennet End lane, but the idea was so incredible. Perry was a gentleman, a buffoon; tiresome, but inoffensive.

Except . . . his jokes were frequently *not* inoffensive. He had asked Rutland about landowners in the county. He was permanently dipped, but continued to gamble. And the Pool had speculated for some time that Flint was getting a lot of his information directly from members of the gentry.

'Thrown her out, have you?' said Perry now, going past with a laugh.

Nick sighed and rolled his eyes at his table companions. 'I daresay he'll become bored with his little joke eventually.'

Ten o'clock was the time when winnings were paid out from the day before. It was noticeable that Viscount Perivale wasn't amongst the first wave of gentlemen who strolled out of the hotel and along the High Street at that hour. The person Nick did see, however, was John Bowman. Now wasn't that a stroke of luck! He put on a turn of speed, brushed alongside the man, then apologised handsomely.

'I beg your pardon,' he said. 'It's Bowman, isn't it? My friend Lord Rothwell introduced us on the heath. My name's Dacre.'

John Bowman looked blank, evidently trying to place him. 'Lord Rothwell? Oh yes, I remember. We were talking about m'sister. Funny, that. I heard from London yesterday; she's engaged to be married! No thought of asking my permission.'

'Congratulations. I trust it is a good match?'

'Gentleman by the name of Congreve; her godmother's son for all. He's an attorney. He's known her for years. You'd think he'd have more sense than to offer for her.'

'Charles Congreve?' said Nick, affecting surprise. 'He's kept that quiet. He's a friend of mine. Good man. Excellent family.'

'Oh yes, nothing wrong with the family, just saying I wouldn't have chosen an attorney for her. Still, she's off my hands now.'

In front of them, Viscount Perivale crossed the road, heading for the coffee house.

John Bowman's face turned a shade redder. 'Him! Do you know him?

'Viscount Perivale?' said Nick. 'Very loose screw.'

'Ha, thought as much,' said Bowman, looking pleased. 'What's he wearing those green ribbons for, eh?'

'A bet, I understand.'

'That so? He bowled up to the house yesterday. I could see he wanted me to ask, so I didn't. Stupid affectation, I call it. Dandyism,' he added disapprovingly.

So it had been Perry in the lane! 'I

entirely agree. I daresay he'd forgotten he was even wearing them. Not the sort of costume I'd go visiting in.'

'Odd sort of cove all round. Never saw him in my life before, then on Monday he says he knows m'sister and asks where she is. And blow me, early yesterday he comes over to Kennet End saying he's heard I've got dogs for sale and he might be interested. Well I have, so I took him down to the kennels but he hardly looked at them. If you ask me, he didn't knew bark from fart. I certainly wasn't going to sell him one. Waste of a good dog.' He eyed Nick appraisingly. 'I don't suppose you'd . . . ?'

'Sadly, I live mostly in London,' said Nick. 'If I spent more time in the country, I might take you up on the offer. How strange of Perivale, though. I wonder what he meant by it?'

'Dashed smoky, I call it. Then he says he must do the pretty by the ladies and he'll come into the house with me to make his bow to my wife!'

Bowman looked so outraged that

Nick murmured, 'And him with green ribbons on his tassels.'

'Well, I mean to say, naturally Mrs Bowman is the sweetest-tempered woman in the world and her refreshments are the equal of anyone's in the county, but it would have been more than my life's worth to invite him in. For one thing, she keeps to her room in the mornings. For another, the man's a viscount! She wouldn't thank me for bringing a viscount into the house without her being prepared for it, now would she?'

'No indeed,' said Nick, much struck. 'Very unhandsome of Perivale to put you in such a position. Were you able to put him off without offence?'

'I said my wife and her mother weren't receiving visitors today and that was that. Off he dashed. I saw him on the heath later and we exchanged nods, so all's well.'

'Quick thinking on your part. Curious though, as you say. Ah, the line is moving at last. The subscription plate will be interesting today, I think. I fancy

Mr Chifney's Romp for it. Nice looking filly.'

They continued to talk about horses until they'd collected their winnings, then Bowman nodded farewell and Nick went thoughtfully towards the livery stables. Viscount Perivale was working for Flint. Their shadow master was extending his reach and no mistake now.

9

'*Once this business is settled, I would like to have the convenience of stabling Satan here.*'

Kitty watched Nicholas leave, that sentence reverberating in her ears. Did he mean when the racing season started again in the spring? He must do, surely. He was only here for this one week and it seemed unlikely that they'd settle anything before then. She brushed cobwebs off her apron, resolutely not thinking about the empty stalls in the stable, or the slim terrace of spare cottages that would be so very suitable for his coachman and grooms. She was reading too much into his words. Their finding comfort in each other during the hours of darkness was all there could ever be. He was a gentleman with a name and a position to keep up, she was a housekeeper with a trail of scandal behind her. And if that didn't make her unsuitable enough, he was dependent on his grandfather. His life was in London, not here.

She turned back slowly, reflecting on how difficult it had been this morning not to touch his hand or lift up her face unthinkingly for a kiss. She must guard against that, keep things friendly and practical. She would be lonely when he left, even with Molly and the others to keep her company. It was easy to say she'd make new friends and reconnect with old ones, but what if the Pool did not discover the person who was after her? She and Ann would be too scared to go out at all.

She stiffened her spine. Well then, they *would* find out. Where had her determination gone? She'd start right now by going through her father's notebook, line by line. There had to be something more than Papa simply getting a name from Mrs Hennessy.

'I'm going back to the house,' she called to Ann, then froze as a carriage pulled in between the gateposts.

Just for a moment, she was unable to move. Flint. Had he found her? Fear beat in her throat. She wanted to call to Ann to hide, but the carriage door was already opening.

Kitty blinked. A lady was being helped down the steps by a solicitous groom. A cheerful, comfortable looking young woman in a pretty bonnet, looking enquiringly around. Kitty hastily untied her apron and went forward. 'May I help you?'

Her visitor's face broke into a delighted smile. 'Kitty? Is it you indeed? Why yes I see it is, for you are just as lovely as you always used to be.'

Kitty found her voice. 'Jenny Rooke? Oh, I beg your pardon, you are Jenny Prettyman now. My felicitations.'

'Thank you. We are all very happy. Adam told me you were here, so I have brought Lottie to meet your daughter and to assure you that if you need a friend, you have one.' Jenny made a comical face at her. 'And yes, I do know this is ridiculously early, but Lottie and I were so very excited about making a morning call like proper visiting ladies, that we thought perhaps you would not mind. We do not make so very many, you see.'

Now Kitty took in the bright, eager, scrubbed face of the eight-year-old scrambling to get out of the carriage behind her stepmother. 'I do not mind at all,' she assured them. 'We have been up several hours because we cannot get used to how quiet it is here, so were just thinking it may be time to stop for a rest.'

The child gave a wide, gap-toothed smile. 'We thought we might not stay clean and tidy if we had to wait too long,' she confided.

Kitty laughed. 'You are going to get on *splendidly* with Ann.' She looked behind her to where her daughter was hanging back shyly. 'We have visitors, Ann. Will you show them into the sitting room while I make some tea and find the seed cake I brought back yesterday? And possibly remove the straw from your hair first?' She glanced at Jenny, who appeared to be the same composed, unflustered person she'd always been, only now with a glow of contentment to her. 'I am afraid as a practice call, Furze House is not ideal for your purposes. I don't have any maids or footmen, and Nicholas has taken the key, so we need to go inside via the kitchen.'

'Think nothing of it,' said her visitor cheerfully. 'I am become much more liberal in my expectations than I used to be. Over the summer I ran away to Adam's touring theatre company. If I had a chair to sit on there, I thought myself fortunate, though hay bales are surprisingly comfortable providing one is wearing stout skirts.'

'Jenny-Mama is very silly sometimes,' said Lottie. 'We had nice chairs, but a house is nicer.' She looked with interest around the kitchen. 'A house with a cook is lovely. Our cook is as fat as butter. Do you have a cook?'

'No, I do the cooking myself. This is my sister's house, really. I am her housekeeper.' She swung the kettle across to the range and busied herself getting out plates and cake, then she and Jenny watched with some tension as the girls very carefully carried them through to the sitting room. They both breathed out at the same time.

'Oh, I am so glad you are back,' said Jenny. 'My friends are splendid, but they are all Verity or Caroline Rothwell's age. It will be nice to have someone nearby who is of my own years. I know we were never especial friends before, but I would like to change that if we may? I was such a mouse in those days, and so envious of you. You were bold and bright and laughing: everything I was not.'

Kitty gave a wry laugh. 'If you are looking for that girl, you will be disappointed. I am so much changed inside I do not recognise myself.'

Jenny took both her hands, and now her eyes were serious. 'That is the other reason I came. We women are much stronger than we ever know, but sometimes we do need help. I will tell you the full story another time, but the reason I concealed myself with the Chartwell Players was that I was in great danger. I know what it is to live with fear from morning to night, to present an untroubled face when you are screaming inside. Adam is the best of men, and he says Mr Dacre is sound and reliable, but gentlemen can never understand our driving concerns. Kitty, if you ever have need of somewhere to keep Ann safe, no matter what time of day or night, bring her to me at Rooke Hall. I will guard her as my own. No one will look for her there.'

Inside her, Kitty felt something break. Jenny Prettyman — even though they had never been close — had arrowed straight to the heart of Kitty's dread and was offering her the single thing she needed. 'Thank you,' she said, a lump in her throat. She hugged the other woman impulsively. 'Thank you.'

It was not the end of the morning's revelations. After what had surely to be the most unconventional call ever, Kitty and Ann were taking leave of their visitors when Nicholas came pelting down the drive.

'Catherine, are you and Ann all right? I saw the carriage and I . . . ' His mouth snapped shut when he saw her in the act of shaking hands. 'I now feel remarkably foolish.'

He cared. Kitty felt a most extraordinary surge of emotion. 'All is well,' she said with a reassuring smile. 'I am more grateful than I can say for your concern, but you do not need to worry. Jenny, may I introduce Nicholas Dacre? Nicholas, this is Adam's wife, Jenny Prettyman. She very kindly brought Lottie to meet Ann. We have all of us been rehearsing morning calls, but I fear we have a considerable way to go before we get them right.'

'Then I beg your pardon for the intrusion. I came back to warn you that the man who was asking your brother about you is Viscount Perivale.'

Kitty's hand went to her breast. 'Perivale? The man who . . . ?' Her eyes darted to the carriage.

'The very same,' said Nicholas, colouring faintly. 'Forgive my disappearing so soon after making your acquaintance, Mrs Prettyman, but I must write a rapid letter to London and then get up to the heath. I daresay we will meet again.' He inclined his head in a bow, then hurried inside.

Jenny's gaze followed him with interest. 'I have never heard of Viscount Perivale, but I will pass the name to Adam,' she said, then pressed Kitty's hand. 'Don't forget my offer.'

Kitty waved them off, prudently sent Ann to Molly and went into the house to find Nicholas. 'What does it mean?' she asked.

He was just sealing his letter, pressing his ring into the wax and rocking it slightly. 'It means we wrought better than we knew in the carriage on Saturday. This adventure could have been over there and then. It also means Flint has his hooks into more of the gentry than the Pool have previously suspected. That is what I need to warn them about. If we could but get a line on where he is recruiting people it would aid us greatly.'

'Will identifying Perivale help you to catch Flint?'

'If Perry has met Flint face to face, then yes it must be of use. If he hasn't, then we might at least discover his modus operandi. We won't know until we have had a little talk with him, and I am not risking that in Newmarket, not with you so close.' He flushed. 'I also think it had better not be me who does the talking. I am too likely to rend the man limb from limb.'

A treacherous warmth spread though Kitty. On its heels came a warning bell. She would have to tell him soon, before he became too fond of her. 'I might know Viscount Perivale by sight if he ever played cards with Simon,' she said guardedly, 'but I do not recognise the name.'

'He is currently sporting green ribbons to his boots, but I beg you will not wander down the street inspecting gentlemen's footwear to see if you are familiar with him.'

'I will not stir beyond the gates, I promise.'

'Thank you. Even so, I wish I was not promised to Rutland this evening.' He picked up his letter, hurried to the door, then turned. 'Damn it,' he muttered. Two strides later he was crushing her to him and kissing her. 'Take great care of yourself,' he said. Then he was gone.

Kitty's knees buckled. She sat abruptly, her fingers pressed to her mouth, feeling the pressure of his lips and the hard clasp of his arm around her ribs. This was nonsensical. She knew how she was starting to feel about *him*, but there was nothing special about her. He must have had many casual mistresses over the years. Why would he feel so strongly about her? There could be no future in it. Had she done him a disservice with her offer of comfort?

Her gaze fell on the notebook. She opened it at the beginning and started to read, resolutely detaching her mind from Nicholas's behaviour. In this she was successful. Her eyebrows rose to her hairline as she turned page after page, tallying up the number of guineas her father had spent on Mrs Hennessy. Whatever sort of woman was she? He had been such a rigid, patriarchal man. Mama had called him a monster. What manner of woman could possibly have such an expensive hold over him?

★　★　★

It had been a useful and generally pleasant day, but a long one and Nick was weary of it. He'd had moderate success on the heath, come back to Cheveley with the duke's party, passed Viscount Perivale's name to Alex Rothwell casually while they were circulating before dinner, joined in with the discussions on Nash's new project in London and how it seemed to have hit a run of bad luck, and successfully evaded all talk of his family, bar replying to polite enquiries with the intelligence that his grandfather was pretty stout, thank you.

'Dacre, just the man. Her Grace tells me it was you who found your mother that charming pair of greys she has to her landau.'

Nick stopped calculating how soon he could plead fatigue and depart. Instead he turned with a ready smile to his host. 'I did, yes. They are not the fastest pair in town, but they have a nice temperament and work well together.'

'You don't know of a similar pair, I suppose? Her Grace was very much taken with them when she was driving in the park last week and saw Heloise out for an airing.'

Nick chuckled. 'Her Grace need only wait three months and my mother will decide she would prefer roans, so the greys will be available.'

'Ladies, my dear Dacre, are not

gentlemen. My dear wife has no interest in playing the long game. She'd like them for tooling about here and now.'

'I can sympathise with that. I could certainly oblige — indeed I have two pairs of my own currently stabled at Whittlesford that may be suitable — but I confess I am puzzled. Surely your own man would not find it too arduous a problem to solve?'

'In the normal way, yes. As a judge of horseflesh, there is no one better. You though, you're good with matching cattle. You've got an eye for it. Your team of chestnuts is superb. There aren't many who have the skill. Her Grace would be delighted to have a Dacre-matched pair. I'd make it worth your while.'

A Dacre-matched pair. At the duke's words, a dazzling idea lit up Nick's mind, nebulous, but glorious. Could he make it work?

'Then how can I refuse?' he said. 'I am honoured at your trust. Are you looking for a quiet pair? Lively? Is it just for the landau or might her Grace drive them herself in the curricle?'

The Duke of Rutland laughed. 'You had best talk to her yourself.' He took Nick by the elbow and steered him across the room. 'My dear, I have the answer to your prayers.'

'Goodness,' said the rather starched matron standing next to the duchess. She appraised Nick through her lorgnette. 'I had no idea you had such a modern marriage.'

★　★　★

The first night had been for him, the second night most definitely for her. After this morning, Kitty judged it best that Nicholas did not arrive home only to be invited straight into her bed. She was not sure for his future peace of mind that there *should* be a third night. She was therefore reclining on the sofa in the sitting room when she heard the front door open. She had her stepmother's grey silk morning dress spread across her lap and was shortening it to fit by pulling it up into a flounce around the hem. The task was sufficiently challenging that it gave her no room to think about what she needed to say.

Nicholas stood in the doorway for a moment, easy and relaxed. Evidently the evening had been a convivial one. 'If that gown is for you, I cannot like the colour,' he said.

She cast him a quick smile. 'It would not be my first choice, but I can fashion rosebuds out of ribbon and affix them to the top of each flounce to lighten it. It will make an unremarkable costume, which is all I want. Additionally, it will be something different to this one I have on, which is also what I want.'

'With your colouring you should wear dusky pinks or deep yellows. Or perhaps that red silk shawl from your father's desk.'

That reminded her of something else. She pushed the grey silk to one side, swinging her legs off the sofa and crossing to the table. 'Ah, no, I have a far better notion for how we can use that. That silk shawl, let me tell you, was the last gift Papa bought for Mrs Hennessy, which is why it was hidden in his desk. He died before he could give it to her.' She handed him the notebook, pointing at the final entry. 'See? It cost thirty guineas. Thirty guineas! Do you not think she would be prepared to exchange the name of Will Lawrence's highwayman for it?'

Nicholas whistled. 'She might indeed.' His gaze travelled over the page. 'She seems to have been a remarkably expensive woman.'

'I daresay John is already congratulating himself because the Kennet End income goes so much further than it did previously. It is only gifts though. No rent on the house. No servant's wages. No allowance. So unless she sold the gifts when low on funds, she must have some other income. If that was my list of requirements in return for favours, it would be far more practical. *Rib of beef, two shillings . . . Brace of pigeons, one-and-thruppence . . .* Nicholas, I have to tell you something.'

He wasn't listening to her. 'You sell yourself too short. How about a fine cod's head? We had one this evening at Cheveley, dressed in a white sauce with peppercorns and, I think, mace.'

'I will look it up in my book to make when I am rich. Nicholas . . . '

'Or if you are in the mood for alternative gifts, what about . . . what about an acre of land for grazing?'

She stared at him, dumfounded. His eyes were luminous and he was plainly paying only lip service to her words. What sort of strange mood was he in? 'Why, pray, would I want an acre of land for grazing?' she asked.

He caught her to him, laughing. 'I will tell you. I have had an enlightening evening. It may yet change my life. But first . . . '

She was helpless in the face of his good spirits, delighted that he was happy and ridiculously gratified that he wanted to share his exuberance with her. She lifted her lips to his, drowning in his kiss.

* * *

'What were you going to say?' he asked, much later.

They had, naturally, progressed to her bed. She was drowsy and warm and felt entirely content. Her carefully prepared speech of earlier belonged in a different life. 'I will tell you tomorrow,' she replied. 'Whatever happened to you this evening? I have never seen you like this.' *So free and uninhibited. So joyous. As if there was another person inside that you were always supposed to be.*

He turned, lean and warm against her, and lay on his back. 'I sold a pair of carriage horses. Two of the team we used on the middle stage of our journey. I will send my groom down to Whittlesford for them tomorrow. Catherine, the Duke of Rutland offered me double what I paid. He said the duchess would be delighted with a Dacre-matched pair.'

She was bewildered. What was there in that to raise him up into the clouds? 'That's good, isn't it?'

He threaded his arm around her shoulders. 'It is very good. It is what I like to do, select horses and match them up to work together. I have sold pairs before, to people who have seen them on my curricle and made me an offer. I have twice sold teams of four, but until his Grace described what he wanted as *Dacre-matched* as if it was a coveted appellation, I had not thought the skill might be something I could turn to account.'

'I don't think I understand,' said Kitty, still mystified.

'You will when I explain. It has been a hobby to me so far. It gives me satisfaction. I see a promising horse, keep it in mind until I see another and put the pair together. Often, through lack of finance or space in my stable, I miss out. What if I went at it with more application? What if I bought horses when I saw them? What if I actively looked for matches? What if I had people in mind who would purchase a particular pair? What if I were to buy promising yearlings, train them up for carriage work myself and match them? I can show them off as I do now and then sell them on.'

Her brow wrinkled. 'You are thinking of this as a business?' She could see problems with this. She wondered if he had seen them too. 'It is an attractive idea. Whether it would be enough to support you, only you can tell. But Nicholas, you live in London. Where would you keep these horses?'

He hugged her joyously. 'Here,' he said. 'I would keep them here.'

For her? Was this because of her? Consternation swamped her, but still for the life of her she couldn't bear to destroy his enthusiasm. 'What of your grandfather?' she managed instead.

His voice flattened. 'Ah, there's the rub. I can hear the old tyrant now. '*A horse-coper, Nicholas? A common* peddler? *Do try to remember what is due to your name.'* I would have to present it in a less workaday light. As a superior service for the gentry. But Catherine, this is where today's commission from the Duke of Rutland has opened my eyes. If my grandfather could be brought to see that *Dacre-matched* is a badge of quality, he would be more inclined to tolerate it. He might even be persuaded to invest. To answer your earlier question, no, the scheme is unlikely to support me, but it gives me a purpose — and it also gives me a valid reason to return here all year round.'

To return to me? To be with me? Or simply to be away from his dreadful family? Kitty was still staring into the darkness as she felt him fall asleep.

★　★　★

'So there it is. He has convinced himself he wants to stay here, and I dare not ask if is partly due to me, because there cannot ever be a future in it.'

Molly blew out her cheeks reflectively. They had fetched bread and milk and a scrag end of mutton for today's pot ('It was a good night,' Molly had said by way of explanation) and were walking slowly back to the house. Kitty was wrapped in her cloak on the inside as usual, shrinking even closer to the wall on the stretch past the White Hart where Viscount Perivale was presumably asleep upstairs.

Molly glanced at her. 'You've not told him about . . . ?'

Kitty swallowed. 'No, but I must. I thought to do it today.'

'Normally I'd say gather in the good moments to see off the bad, but if he's sweet on you, it won't do to keep stuff like that from him.'

'I know, and when I do, that will be an end to it. No gentleman wants my history in a mistress.' *Things once done*. Wasn't that what he had said? 'You'd think I would know better, wouldn't you?' she went on. 'And I do, for at first it was just comfort for both of us. You know how it is.'

'None better.'

'But now I . . . '

'You're sweet on him too?'

Kitty nodded. 'He is a good man, for all his reputation. He is scarred himself. I don't know why; there is more to it than just his family. That isn't it, though. I feel . . . you will think me very sentimental, but I feel he is mine to take care of. I can't bear to withdraw a source of comfort from him. I don't want to tear away a place where he can find peace.'

'I was right then; he is one of the lonely ones?'

'You are not generally wrong about men.'

'I've seen enough of them. I was right about pockets-to-let Perivale too, wasn't I? Doesn't surprise me Flint's got his hooks into him. I doubt he'll know much. He's not as clever as your Sim. Cat's paw, that's all. Makes you think though, doesn't it? He was around the inns last night. Made out he was after something on account, but they all know it's money on the table. What he *did* want was to know what I was doing so far from home and how long I'd been here. I told him I came up with a gentleman a few weeks ago who went back without me. I said I'd taken a fancy to the town and it was healthier than London. He gave a funny sort of laugh at that and said it was likely to be healthier for me than it was for him. I pretended to think he meant the betting on the horses and said the legs and gullgropers were always the real winners.'

Kitty looked at her, dismayed. 'Oh Molly, I hope he doesn't report to Flint that you are here.'

'I don't see it. I made out it was partly all my favourite gentlemen visiting the town so often that had tempted me to stay on. He's got eyes, he could see it was true that I wasn't short of company. Like I said, he's not that clever. He's fixed on himself and his woes. That's what would have made me suspicious even if you hadn't tipped me the wink. They all know I can't be doing with anything but plain dealing, no matter what story they come up with.'

'I hope you are right. I would hate to think I had drawn you all into danger.'

'We'll be snug enough. I daresay your Mr Dacre and his friends will deal with Viscount Perivale before ever he gets near London. Oh, and talking of the lonely ones, I had a right lost soul yesterday. Old story: his wife not interested any more, doesn't pay him as much attention as she used to, bound up with her ma, absorbed in stuff that don't concern him, always tired, that sort of thing. Well, I said I'd oblige, but it turns out he's local, so he had to get a private parlour and then wedge a chair across the door. Still, he was very grateful and fancied talking as much as finding some relief. It wasn't until the end I tumbled to the fact that his wife's increasing! Well, I said, no wonder she's not interested, you great lummox. It'll all be right and tight when the babe's born. You get home and rub her back for her.'

Kitty raised her eyebrows. 'She is lucky to get away with putting him off. I never could.'

'Ah well, here we are, and here's your man looking for you.'

Kitty braced herself. 'I'll talk to him today. Can you keep Ann with you again? I believe we are to go to Bury St Edmunds.'

'Safe as the Bank of England. Never fret. Give me your basket, I'll put it indoors.' She bustled inside, leaving Kitty to greet Nicholas.

'Good morning.'

He smiled at her. 'I was going to look over the stables. Do you care to join me?'

'Certainly. You are still of the same mind as last night regarding your venture?'

'Yes, if it is feasible. Who owns the land next door, do you know?'

'I have no idea, but it seems unused.

Mrs Green might be able to tell you. Shall we ask her? If not, Jenny and Adam have space at Rooke Hall. Jenny said Adam was thinking to hire out some of their fields.'

Mr & Mrs Green were at the end of the vegetable plot, looking across the lane towards the common field. Mr Green greeted them morosely.

'Rabbits,' he said. 'Coming over here eating my carrots.' He ran the slingshot he was carrying between his fingers. 'Can't set a trap for 'em. 'It isn't allowed on the common land.'

'And if you did, that Ned Tucker'd have the coney afore you got to it,' said Mrs Green. She sent a brooding look across to where half a dozen rabbits were grazing in the autumn sunshine. 'Shame, I call it. I do like a bit of rabbit stew.'

'Are you going to try for one?' Nicholas asked Mr Green, indicating his sling.

Mrs Green huffed. 'He won't get it. Eyes aren't what they used to be.'

'May I try?' asked Kitty. 'I used to be a tremendous shot.'

Mr Green seemed dubious, but his wife nudged him and he handed the sling over. Kitty tested the weight at the end, looped it between finger and thumb, fitted a pebble to the pouch just as if she'd last done it yesterday instead of ten years ago and took aim. The pebble flew swift and smooth through the air.

'Got it, mum! Well, I'll be . . . ' Belying his years, the elderly gardener scuttled through the gate and clambered over the rail to the common grazing, intent on retrieving the luckless rabbit.

Kitty handed the sling back to Mrs Green. 'Enjoy your meal. Next time I must be sure to have a couple of pebbles ready. I remember now there is generally time to get in two fast shots before they all scatter.' She grinned at Nicholas who was regarding her with astonishment. 'Shocked?'

'Impressed. Are you as good with a pistol?'

She shook her head. 'I have never

had sufficient practice. Stones are freely available. One doesn't waste shot handing it over to mere females.'

Nicholas obtained the name of the agents for the unused land and they returned to the stable.

'Molly thinks Fred will arrive today,' continued Kitty. 'She was propositioned by Viscount Perivale last night but declined on account of not being charity-minded. She says he is known as 'pockets-to-let' on the streets.'

'That's interesting. Rolled up, is he? Hopefully he will be trying to remedy it on the heath today. I think we should risk taking the carriage to Bury St Edmunds. It will give my coachman something to do. I'll send Thomson down to Whittlesford to collect one pair of the greys. Can you be ready in an hour?'

'Easily. Nicholas, I am worried about Viscount Perivale. He was asking Molly how long she has been in Newmarket and why she came. She told him she arrived with a racing gentleman some time ago and decided to stay, and naturally she wouldn't breathe a word about me, but Flint is not stupid. If Perivale *does* mention Molly when he returns . . . '

Nicholas's whole bearing became infinitely more dangerous. 'We will take steps to ensure he doesn't.'

10

It was a matter of fifteen miles to Bury St Edmunds and a pleasant, autumnal day for a drive. As they passed the turning to Kennet End, Nick couldn't help catching Catherine's eye. She returned him a preoccupied smile.

'What are you thinking?' he asked.

Her reply surprised him. 'That I do not know you. By which I mean although I know you very well at the most personal level, I do not know the rest. For instance, I do not know how you fit into the outside world.'

I don't. Not at all. 'I prefer not to think of the outside world when I am at Newmarket. Here I am free of family, and in that I am no different to a score of younger sons — or the sons of younger sons, to be more accurate. Do you wish to know more?'

'I should like to, if you have no

objection to telling me. There is a danger to lo . . . living in isolation.'

He picked up the stumble. *Loving?* Had she been going to say loving? An unfamiliar sensation swirled around his chest. He was conscious of a reluctance to continue. 'I warn you, my story is not pretty.'

'Nor is mine. I suppose I am hoping to get an idea of how you might receive it.'

'A tale for a tale, then?'

She shook her head. 'Mine is not conditional. I must tell you anyway. But I should like to know your history.'

Nick felt as if his valet had just inserted him into a lead waistcoat instead of the figured silk he'd been expecting. This had had to come, he supposed. He had been playing at independence at Furze House, a person in his own right. But the way he was starting to feel about Catherine, she deserved to know the worst, though the knowledge would do neither of them any good. He sighed and started further back than he needed to, purely to prolong the time they had left.

'My grandfather is a despot. He neither seeks nor gives affection. Everything — property, land and money — is in his hands alone. No entails, no obligations. What he dribbles out, he exacts a high price for. My eldest uncle manages the main estate as I have told you; my second eldest is in the church with a family living and not enough money from it to propel himself upwards in the hierarchy. My third uncle escaped to the regular army with the proviso that he first marry an insipid heiress in order to bolster the purse of the smaller estate where she now lives.'

'A despot, as you say.'

'Indeed, and then there are my numerous cousins, all equally dependent on him for favours and advancement. Family gatherings are more akin to wars of attrition than celebrations. One is constantly checking one's back.'

'I can see why you would grow armour. What of your own branch?'

Now they came to it. 'My mother, whom Society refers to as *la belle Heloise* almost certainly, with her own connivance, escaped from France just before the Terror. Her family lost their lands. Her parents lost their lives.'

Catherine's eyes grew wide. 'That's awful.'

'It caused her to cling to whatever she could find. She captivated my father and rushed him down the aisle before he could draw breath.'

'I can understand that.'

'After first telling the eminently suitable and *not* insipid heiress he was engaged to that Society was laughing at the unfortunate woman behind her back because Heloise herself was having a tumultuous affaire with the heiress's betrothed.'

'Oh, that's not so understandable.'

'It had the desired effect. Exit heiress, enter *la belle Heloise* in robes of glory. My father died when I was very young. There are moments when I think it was out of self-defence. My mother instantly declared her heart was broken, and nothing would prevent her from being a devoted prop to my grandfather in his hour of grief. She has been a devoted prop for some twenty-five years now, having fought, slashed and bitten her way into running his house and being the consummate hostess whenever he entertains.'

'What she has, she holds,' murmured Catherine.

'What she has, she wraps in three layers of chains and four padlocks,' corrected Nick. 'She kept me at home as long as she could, not because she had a fondness for me or because I was often struck down with feverish maladies as a child, but because it strengthened her position in the household. The day we met, you said you would do anything for your daughter. She would do anything for herself.'

Catherine bit her lip. 'Even so, to lose everything, to lose her parents . . . '

'This is what she traded on. It would be more tragic had she not saved herself by telling the soldiers who found her that there were aristocrats in the cart behind.'

'Nicholas!' She looked at him in shock.

'Just so. Your father had his rival in love murdered. My mother sacrificed her own parents. I may be wronging her, of course. She only told me that part of the story once, in French when I was quite young. She may have intended it as an exciting bedtime tale. Needless to say, I failed to sleep for several weeks.'

She took his hand. 'How did you grow up so nice?'

'I am not nice. Ask anyone.'

'I do not need to ask them. I have the evidence of my own eyes.'

He grinned and traced a pattern on her palm, wondering if he could buy her a new pair of gloves without giving offence. 'Severe reaction, I think. Or possibly my father had the only generous traits in the family and contrived to pass them on to me. And then I met Charles, of course. He was always very hot on justice for all. Fortunately, apart from telling me scary stories about escaping from France and refusing to let me go to school until my grandfather forcibly tore me away from her potions and tinctures and threw me into the carriage with my trunk strapped on the roof, my mother had little to do with my upbringing. My consolation is that she and my grandfather deserve each other. They are both shallow and mercurial. He exists on power. She glories in position and possessions. All his daughters-in-law are similar, even the insipid one who has developed a complaining whine that can penetrate solid oak. It is a battle of epic proportions when they come together.'

'It all sounds horrific.'

'My grandfather thrives on it, especially when all my cousins are there too. He enjoys setting one against another. My mother is planning fireworks in the gardens for his birthday ball. I promise you it will be as nothing to the fireworks inside.'

And he would have to be back for the

occasion and do the pretty and continue to live a lie. When he contrasted the senseless, stifling battles of wit in his grandfather's house with the gloriously healthy open-air vision of life he'd glimpsed yesterday it made him even more determined to give it a try. He knew his will was as strong as his grandfather's. This was the first time he'd had a compelling enough reason to exercise it to the limit. He stole a glance at Catherine. She was shocked, but crucially she didn't seem repulsed by him, even knowing what had gone into his ancestry. She was even still holding his hand.

She sat up straighter as the first Bury St Edmunds houses came into view. Basely, Nick decided to save the rest of his disclosure. He wanted to hold on to the dream a little longer before his lustrous new palace of cards came crashing down around him.

★ ★ ★

They drove slowly up Northgate Street with Catherine looking intently out of the window. 'There it is,' she said. 'I am sure that is the house. Do you see it? It still has a blue front door, though it looks freshly painted. Shall we call now or leave the carriage at the Angel Hotel and walk back?'

Nick kept his eye on the house. A man in his middle years advanced up the steps, knocked and was admitted by a smart maid. 'The Angel, and I think you had better wait there also,' he said. 'It strikes me that the mistress of the house might respond better to a male visitor than a female.'

'I imagine there is very little doubt of it,' replied Catherine. 'May I wait for you in the print shop opposite instead? The choicest items of news are always to be found in such places.'

He chuckled. 'Although possibly not quite as accurate as in a newspaper.' It was another way in which Catherine differed from the Dacre females. They would have demanded he conduct them to the modiste before he went anywhere himself.

Once he had seen her into the shop, Nick took the red silk shawl in its matching bag and prepared to cross the road. The gentleman he had noticed arriving was just taking his leave, not walking quite as nimbly or looking quite as dapper as previously. Mrs Hennessy was evidently a lady of some dispatch.

'Good day,' said Nick to the pert maid who opened the door. 'I should like to see Mrs Hennessy, if you please.' He flipped a shilling between his fingers as he spoke.

The maid looked him up and down with considerable interest. As accustomed as he was to being ogled by the fairer sex, Nick nevertheless felt his face heating.

'What name shall I give?' she asked at length, holding out her hand for his gloves, hat and the shilling.

He smiled at her. 'Mr Smith.'

The room where he was received was

heavy with swags of crimson velvet and rich with the scent of beeswax, wine and spices. There was a cushioned couch along one wall with a painting of quite astonishing anatomical endeavours hanging above it. As if this wasn't enough, a single glance at the woman by the window told Nick exactly why Mr Bowman senior had kept returning. Tall and handsome, well past middling years, she exuded sex and strong discipline in equal measures. It was as if one's strictest governess had walked into the schoolroom dressed in nothing but furs, whipcord and an if-you're-very-very-good expression. Nick felt an urgent need to stand up straight and simultaneously loosen his neckcloth.

'Well?' she said in a voice that combined sumptuous velvet with the crack of leather. 'What can I do for you, Mr Smith?'

Nick strove for an aristocratic drawl. 'It is more a case of what you can do for yourself. I was given your name by the late Mr Bowman.'

The woman's eyes instantly flicked to the silk bag he carried. 'Were you now? Poor John. I was powerfully sad to hear he'd passed away.'

Having seen Mr Bowman's notebook, Nick could very easily believe that to be the truth. 'I am working with the family,' he said. 'He was accustomed to bring you . . . gifts.'

'He was a generous man,' she murmured, letting her gaze run over him. 'I frequently had to chastise him for spending too much. The more he spent, the more I chastised him. How about you, Mr Smith? Is there anything you do that you should be punished for?' She ran her fingers lightly down a switch lying next to the decanter on a side table.

Nick repressed a strong urge to edge backwards. 'Unlike the late Mr Bowman, my conscience is entirely clear. He did, however, leave a last gift. I will let you have it in return for just one thing.'

She smiled. 'Certainly.'

Not that, you mantrap. 'Twenty years ago John Bowman desired an unusual service. You gave him a name. Might I have that name, please?'

For the first time, Mrs Hennessy looked startled. 'Sure, why would a healthy young gentleman like yourself need to know such a thing?'

'Natural curiosity, madam.' He swung the bag idly.

Her eyes followed it, weighed him up, revised her first opinion. 'It was my brother who helped him out,' she said, her manner markedly more business-like. 'It'll not profit you any though, for he's been hanged these five years. Sad disgrace to the family, though I always had a soft spot for him and would put commissions his way when I could. Ah, my poor Patrick. He cheated the gallows once, but when he was captured in the very act of holding up the local magistrate's new coach, it was bellows to mend with him.'

He cheated the gallows once. Nick tried to keep any alertness out of his voice. 'I can see that would prove difficult to explain away. How did he escape the hangman the first time?'

'He traded secrets. I wouldn't know who with. He said he'd done a deal with a man that was set to hand him over. He stayed with me whenever his fancy brought him in this direction, but he had powerful restive feet. I don't doubt that's why he took to the road that last time. We always knew he'd be walking up the wooden hill at the end. It was just a matter of when.'

Having got the name, passed over the shawl and declined an offer of favours at special rates, Nick escaped to the street where he took several deep breaths of uncontaminated air before crossing the road to find Catherine.

★ ★ ★

Kitty watched Nicholas in awe as he laced a cup of the Angel Hotel's coffee with brandy, drank it straight down and then poured himself another. 'I have the name she gave your father,' he said. 'It was her own brother.'

'What did you have to do for it?' she couldn't help asking.

He gave a shamefaced grin. 'Only stay in the same room as her for long enough. It appears your lord-of-all-he-surveyed father was in thrall to a lady whipster.'

'No! I cannot believe it.'

'You would, had you been in that boudoir. The power coming from her was immense — and wrong. I was glad to leave.'

'I wonder if that was why he was so tyrannical at home? Taking it out on us where he was master, because she made him feel helpless, yet he could not prevent himself from returning.'

'I do not pretend to know about the human psyche.'

'How about human frailties?'

'Oh, I know about them. I have a number of them myself. Which particular frailty concerns you?'

'Vanity. I should very much appreciate visiting the haberdashers while we are here and buying some cheerful ribbon for the grey dress.'

He smiled. 'That sounds a pleasantly healthy diversion. Mrs Hennessy's brother was apparently hanged five years ago, but let me write a letter to Fitz so Charles may start tracing him anyway, and then I am all yours.'

Oh, if only that were the case. Kitty applied herself hastily to the coffee pot that her yearning might not show on her face.

His letter did not take long. He folded it, wrote the direction and then sealed it with a wafer of wax. As she had seen him do before, he tugged off his bloodstone ring and pressed it to the hot wax to make the seal.

'May I see?' she asked. 'What is the design?'

'My grandfather's crest. A tower, with an eagle; can you make it out? Curse it, the wax was not warm enough — some has got stuck in the intaglio.'

'I have a pin. I will clean it out while you see about posting your letter.'

But he returned almost immediately

with the intelligence that the landlord was most apologetic, but another party had arrived who had previously bespoken the parlour, so Kitty quickly dropped the ring into her reticule for safe keeping and they sallied forth into the town.

'It is a novelty to be purchasing something to use, rather than an item chosen to fetch the best price in the pawn shop,' she said, looking around the haberdashery counters. 'It was the only way I could save money from Simon, by converting it into what he called frippery.'

Nicholas looked down at her, amused. 'And what did you call it?'

'Dinner,' she replied. 'I apologise. I will lighten the mood by buying ribbon for Ann and for Molly's girls too. Oh . . . '

'What is it? What have you seen?'

Kitty's eyes had been drawn to the cards of cord. She glanced mischievously at him. 'Mentioning dinner has reminded me. Six yards of the thin yellow cord, please. Thank you.'

'You are going to use golden cord to

truss up a hen?'

She chuckled. 'No, to pot a rabbit. After this morning's success, I have a fancy to braid myself a sling. I used to make very good ones when I was younger. I hope I have not lost the way of it.'

'You are a woman of unexpected talents. Will you allow me to pay for these purchases?'

'Thank you, and should I be lucky, you can congratulate yourself on having a hand in the supper.'

'Then as a reward, might I also add a pair of warmer gloves for you? These you have on are near falling apart.' When she hesitated, he added, 'I promise you are the least expensive lady I have ever accompanied to a shop like this.'

Kitty bit her lip. The gloves might be the one and only gift he would ever give her. He had told her his story in the carriage on the way here. She should tell him hers on the way back. 'I shall be glad of them,' she said quietly.

'Thank you again.'

But once in his coach on the way back to Newmarket, Nicholas reverted to speculation on how he could best present his horse-matching scheme to his grandfather.

Kitty listened, knowing she was putting off the moment. 'Will he advance you money for purchases?'

'For horses, yes. For housing or other distractions, no. One of his most charming pieces of unsolicited advice was that it costs upwards of three thousand pounds a year to keep a mistress worthy of a gentleman's custom and he wasn't going to advance me that much when I . . . '

'When you what?' she asked when he stopped abruptly.

He seemed to recollect himself. 'Oh, when I wouldn't get any lasting benefit.'

'Is there no benefit in companionship?'

'He does not understand the concept. Companionship for him is someone dependent on him for their daily bread. He feeds on the power.' He shrugged.

'In any case, paid-for companionship is a treacherous illusion. It is better to buy it by the evening, then you are in no danger of confusing it with true affection.'

Free choice, paid for and banked. If only it was always that easy. 'Yes, that is at least an honest transaction,' she said.

'A contract for an hour or two, then you each go your separate ways. I think your friend Molly is a specialist in that. Has there ever been a Mr Turner?'

Kitty gave him a quick smile. 'I do not believe so. She has often said she'd be puzzled to know what to do with a husband if she had one. She adopted the 'Mrs' when it became obvious Dicky was on the way. She is a very practical creature, but not at the expense of hurting others. She told me she met a gentleman yesterday who wanted her company because he felt neglected at home. Through conversing with him, she realised he hadn't appreciated that his wife had changed her habits because she was increasing.

Molly read him a lecture on women's needs and sent him back to pay attention to his lady!'

'Thus cutting off her own source of income?'

'He was only foolish, not flash. If more men understood women, the world would be a more comfortable place.'

'What of you? Do you consider a man ignoring his wife for another to be guilty of poor behaviour?'

She fancied there was a slight constraint in his voice, but answered honestly. If he was minded to judge Molly or her clients, it was none of her business. 'Every case is different, surely? Every gentleman is different. Simon left me alone for weeks whilst he pursued other females, but that was business as he saw it, though there would have been a good deal of pleasure in it for him too. He was another who craved being the centre of attention.'

'Blackguard.'

'Worse than that.' Kitty took a deep

breath. She had put this off long enough. It was time, and it had come upon her unawares. 'He also used me to pay his debts.'

'I beg your pardon?'

She kept her head downbent, focusing her attention on her new gloves. In a painful way, it was a relief that the task of telling him was not now hanging over her.

'Currency, Nicholas. I was currency. The first time was when Ann was still a baby. I told you, I think, that Simon came back a few weeks after the birth with money in his pocket. Wherever he had been, it had given him a distaste for Water Street, for which I was grateful. We moved to nicer rooms, there was money for food and new clothes. It lasted maybe eight months. Then . . . ' She drew a ragged breath. 'Then Simon arrived home one afternoon with a man I had never seen before. A soldier. A captain, I think. Simon pointed at me, said the bedroom was through that door and sat down to wait.'

Nicholas had been leaning back against the squabs. Now he sat up in disbelief and tilted her chin so he could look into her face. His own was horrified. 'Dear God, Catherine . . . '

'I was so numb,' she said, her voice bleak. 'So scared. I couldn't believe it was happening. The soldier pushed me on to the bed, thrust a couple of times and left. Afterwards, Simon said he'd owed him money from gambling and, because the regiment was being deployed the next day, I was the only way to pay him. I must see it was a debt of honour.'

'Honour!'

'*His* honour. My own didn't come into it.'

Nicholas swore fluently. 'I dearly wish your husband was not already dead. I would have done Flint's work for him with pleasure.' He stared out of the window, fists clenched.

Kitty made herself continue. 'Simon's big fear was the thought of physical violence being done to him. He had a horror of it. That had to have come from the army, else he would scarce have joined up. In the years before he routinely began to play with marked cards, the threat of a beating made using me a much more palatable resort when he was pressed to pay his debts. The more he did it, the easier it became for him. Believe me, I learned to look forward to his visits to the country very much.' Her voice faltered. 'Not all his creditors were as straightforward as the soldier.'

Nicholas grasped her hands tightly. 'Never again,' he vowed, and his eyes were dark and implacable as he looked into hers. 'Never again will you be abused. Never again will you be used as a man's property. I swear, Catherine. I swear I will protect you.'

But he would not always be here. And he would no longer lie with her. He would be nauseated. 'There is one more thing to tell you,' she said. 'But here we are passing the church and besides . . . ' *The rest of the tale needs wine in my belly and a place where I can curl up alone and forget.*

'Later,' he said. 'Out you get. I will take the carriage to the White Hart for now, and then show my face on the heath.' He kissed her. 'This makes no difference.'

Not yet. Not until you have had time to think about it. Not until you hear the rest.

11

She had told him. Kitty watched the carriage disappear around the corner of the lane and felt as though she was saying goodbye. The thin October sun was cold on her skin, and the wind from the east penetrated through the fabric of her gown. Only her hands were warm, the evidence of his care. Oh, in the shock of the moment Nicholas might claim her history made no difference, but no man wants shoddy goods, not even in a mistress. In half an hour he would be back on the heath, mixing with his friends, men of rank and fortune. In his own world again. Her small, shabby life could not even come close. She drew a painful breath. She had best see to putting the gentlemen's wing of Furze House in order, ready for when he returned in the spring. They would revert to being housekeeper and guest.

It would be easier for him if he didn't have to see her so often. Life would go on. It always had.

Bracing herself to appear normal, she opened the back gate — and walked into as much confusion as she had been accustomed to see every day in the crowded London courtyards. The only difference was that in Covent Garden there were tall walls surrounding them on all sides, whereas here everything was open to the wide Suffolk skies.

Within a minute, she ascertained the cause of the commotion. Fred Grimes and Dick Turner had arrived and all Molly's family had turned out to greet them, get an account of how Dicky had comported himself on the journey, unload the hackney carriage, display the laundry building, show Fred his cottage and make a fuss of his patient mare. Kitty shook hands too, satisfied herself that Ann was happy and involved in the bustle, then left them to it, saying she would see to today's meal.

She was glad to be alone. Telling over

her past to Nicholas had brought too many memories crowding into her mind. She needed to pack them away again. To bury them some place where they could no longer shame her. To take comfort in her pretty sitting room. To busy herself with meat and onions and potatoes. To stew apples and add a pinch of spice and make pastry for a pie. To create something satisfying and delicious out of nothing, instead of destroying this fragile new life she'd been building.

To resolutely not think of Nicholas saying that what she had told him made no difference. It was sweet of him. And noble. And impossible.

★　★　★

'I have received a letter from Fitz,' said Alex Rothwell, his attention on the runners for the next race and, if his hand gestures were anything to go by, comparing Lord Jersey's bay colt to Mr Stonehewer's brown filly. 'Billy the landlady's boy is safe in deepest Norfolk. I

266

didn't know the Fitzgilbert empire had an outpost on the coast, did you?'

Nick wrenched his mind back from Catherine and what she had told him. 'I vaguely remember him mentioning it one time.'

'Less happily, another wretched woman has been found dead in the Thames, beaten and bruised in the same way as the others.'

'Damnable,' said Nick in disgust. 'We must track whichever sick mind is doing this and stop them. It is unbelievable that nobody ever has information. There is as much silence on the subject as we run up against when we try following anything to do with Flint.'

'A bundle dropped by night into the water of the docks? Who is going to admit to seeing that?'

'Better watchmen are needed. Can you not get an Act passed in Parliament?'

'I wish it were that simple. This communication between us, incidentally, will be a good deal easier when your new venture becomes established.

Caroline charged me with letting you know she has a remarkably pretty chestnut filly that would be just the thing for a lady's carriage. Any time you would like to come over to the Penfold Lodge paddocks to inspect her, you will be more than welcome.'

Nick's jaw dropped. 'How in heaven's name does your wife know anything about it? The duke only commissioned me to find him a pair of greys just last night.'

'You ask that of Caro? She talks to the grooms. They were full of the news this morning. *Dacre-matched*, they are calling it.'

'And all before I have even approached my grandfather for funding!'

'Caro is very pleased. She hates selling the non-racers to people who won't look after them properly.'

'Oh well, that settles it. I shall close with Prettyman on the hire of a couple of his fields immediately. Tell me, do the grooms have an opinion on whether I am likely to succeed?'

'Odds on, apparently. Ho, they're off. I'll see you later.'

Nick followed more slowly. *Dacre-matched* was established fact already? A feeling of warmth stole through him. Warmth and pride. The approbation of the stable-hand brotherhood was not something to be taken lightly.

He realised he had missed the finish of the race, but by the looks of it, Lord Jersey had won. He backtracked to the Running Gap where the next race would start and saw Daniel Chesterfield looking querulous. He was keeping his seat on one of the White Hart hacks with difficulty.

'Your mount's restive,' commented Nick, coming up alongside.

'Perry had her out yesterday, off God knows where,' said Chesterfield peevishly. 'It's my belief he's lamed her.'

Nick studied the mare's gait. 'She looks sound to me, but the girth could do with tightening. Hold fast and I'll see to it.' He dismounted from Satan who stood steady as a rock while Nick tightened the strap.

'He's well trained,' said Chesterfield, a trace of discontent in his tone. 'How much do you want for him?'

More than you can afford. 'Sorry, Satan's not for sale. He suits my image too well.' He looked around. 'All alone today?'

'Richards was as green as a bowl of peas this morning and Perry's gone off somewhere again. It's too bad. He hustled us into coming up here Saturday night instead of Sunday as we'd planned, then we hardly see him all week.'

'Very shabby behaviour.' *Where else had Perivale been? Still haunting Kennet End?* He was fairly sure he hadn't been following them on the Bury Road.

'Downright poor,' grumbled Chesterfield. 'And he still owes me for his share of the post charges. I wish I'd brought my own cattle now. Thanks for . . . ' he waved vaguely downwards.

Nick mounted again and worked the rest of the heath, taking care to be seen with as many groups as possible. What he really wanted was to hurry back to Furze House and continue his conversation with Catherine. She had been through so much, and he had left her far too abruptly earlier. She was going to be hurt again. He needed to soften what he had to tell her. Unfortunately, escaping from today's races mid-programme would cause exactly the sort of comment he was trying to avoid. Never had he cursed his falsely convivial lifestyle more. The matches now were all single pairs of horses and he bet wrongly in all of them. A waste of an afternoon, he reflected crossly.

He rode back, wrestling with the problem of how to entice Viscount Perivale into a trap so the Pool could have a discussion with him on the subject of his employer. There were so many considerations to take into account that he turned in at the entrance to Furze House without thinking and only realised his error once he had already dismounted and was about to lead Satan into the stable.

Idiot. That's what wool-gathering does for a man's wits. Something in him rebelled at taking Satan back over to the livery stables. Thomson would most likely still be on the road with the greys, and Nick had been going to move Satan here anyway. He'd collect his spare tack later.

Inside the stable, he was brought up short by the sound of a man talking softly. An unfamiliar whinny made Satan prick up his ears.

'Well, old girl, seems snug enough, eh? This journey's been an adventure for both of us, but I don't doubt we're settled now. The field was something like, wasn't it? Abel Green said it was common grazing, but it seems an odd set up. Now, what's got you so . . . ? Oh, good afternoon sir, I didn't see you there. My, that's a prime bit of flesh, that is. You'll be the guvnor then? I'll shift my old girl and you can have this loosebox. Won't take me a quarter hour to fix her up with another one.'

'Please don't put yourself to the

trouble. The truth is, my wits were wandering when I brought Satan in, but if you'll give me a hand, I'll sort out this next box for him. You're Fred Grimes, I take it? My name is Dacre.'

Nick removed his coat and waistcoat as he spoke and lifted the fork down from the wall to pitchfork some straw across.

Fred Grimes was scandalised. 'Here, you don't want to be doing that, and you a gentleman. That's my trade.'

Nick grinned. 'Stand easy. We're all one in the stable. That's what the head groom told me when I was a boy. Even my grandfather — who is the highest man in the instep I have ever known — was adamant that I shouldn't have a pony of my own until I knew how to care for it from the cobbles up.'

'From the cobbles up. That's a good one.' Fred wheezed with laughter. 'Not but what you're right. Here, give me that, do, and you see to getting his tack off. I'm bidden inside for a bit of dinner soon, then I'll keep an eye on your fine lad. Ma Turner said I'd be welcome to sit with them, but me and the boy got used to the quiet on the way up. I daresay Molly will be going out. She knows her own mind, that one, but it won't hurt for her to know I'll be biding out here awhile in case of difficulty. Where's the closest jug and bottle?'

'Two alleys down. You can't miss it.'

Fred nodded. 'And Abel's going to show me where to get the feed tomorrow. We'll settle right in, guvnor.'

Guvnor. He liked that. It sounded . . . right. It gave him a place. Such a small thing to make him feel as if he belonged. He only hoped he still would after he'd said what he had to say to Catherine. 'You'd best set up an account.' Nick fished a couple of sovereigns out of his pocket. 'Tell them Nicholas Dacre, Furze House.'

★　★　★

Kitty was astounded when Nicholas walked through the door. She'd settled with herself that he wouldn't be back until late tonight, and would then go straight to his room. Wondering, hardly daring to hope, she laid two places at the table in the sitting room. 'I can tell you've been with Fred in the stable,' she said, 'but he'd be uncomfortable with you eating your meal in the kitchen with all of them.'

In spite of his protests about not meriting special treatment, she didn't think he was that unhappy with the arrangement. 'As you wish,' he said. 'It smells very good. I'll play butler and open the wine I bought in Bury.' He paused. 'Do we have any wine glasses?'

She chuckled. 'There is a set with the good china in that dining room the size of Hackney. I'll bring a tray in. Are you not going out again this evening?'

He shook his head. 'I would not have gone this afternoon if I hadn't had to. I left you very abruptly.'

He wanted to continue the conversation from the carriage. Kitty had a brief, cowardly moment when she

275

contemplated whisking Ann in here to eat with them instead of leaving her in the noisy cheer of the kitchen.

'By the by,' added Nicholas. 'Alex Rothwell tells me your former landlady's son is now safely in Norfolk.'

And there he went, disconcerting her again with his normality and sheer niceness. 'Oh, that is such a relief,' she said. 'I'll let Molly know. I know she's been worrying.'

She left the room to fetch wine glasses, giving up all attempts to fret herself into nervous exhaustion at the thought of the talk they must have later on, and concentrating instead on the food.

★   ★   ★

'I have looked more closely at the other wing,' she said towards the end of the meal after he had regaled her with his conspicuous lack of success on the heath. 'The rooms are not as bad as Mrs Green gave us to understand, but I think it will all need refurbishment before your friends can use it with any degree of comfort. How long is Lord Fitzgilbert's purse, do you know? And who is to decide on the furnishings?'

Nicholas looked blank for a moment. 'I will ask when I return,' he said. 'Fitz's sister, perhaps. Or Verity. They are close friends.' He cleared his throat. 'If my plans pan out, I will likely be the first guest in there. Is it really so untenable? Ann will have to choose me the best room. I am not sure I should remain in the main house.'

It was what she had been expecting, but hearing the words aloud was still akin to a hammer blow to the heart. 'I understand,' she said quietly.

'You don't. Catherine, this is no reflection on you.'

'Wait.' She stood and started to clear the table. 'There is something very squalid about having a serious conversation while there are dirty plates on the table and the remains of an apple pie that should be back in the pantry for tomorrow.'

He smiled wryly. 'Especially when it is as appetising as that one. I am sorry. I have spoiled an excellent meal. If I could, I would have avoided the talk we must have. I will go outside and check on Satan and stretch my legs for a while.' He caught her hand to his lips. 'Take care of that pie. It is comforting to know that there will be a tomorrow.'

Kitty blinked away her tears as the door closed behind him. Apparently they were still to be friends, even if their brief liaison was over. She should have foreseen that. He was so honourable, he would always consider himself duty-bound to guard her until Viscount Perivale had left Newmarket, whatever his personal feelings might be.

In a positive light, the removal of any hope of future intimacy made it easier to tell him the rest. A trickle of thankfulness touched her that she had not committed the folly of telling him in words how she felt about him. Rejection after that would have been very difficult to bear. Even so, her heart still misgave her when she thought about his lonely state.

She cleared up, got Ann to bed and made a pot of tea which she carried on a tray back to the sitting room. The wine had paved the way, now she needed the comfort of warmth.

Nicholas had returned while she'd been occupied. He had made up the fire and angled the sofa closer to it. As she entered, he took the tray from her and set it down. Then he lifted his glass of wine and stared into its ruby depths. 'Catherine, this is not going to be easy.'

She stopped him. 'Please. I know you have planned a gentle, reasonable explanation of why it is no longer appropriate for us to . . . ' She broke off. 'I am saying this badly. You heard only half of my story earlier. The rest is important for the Pool, but it brings so many memories that it is not something I can recount unless my courage is high. May I be very selfish and finish? Before you say anything. Before you explain your position.'

'Believe me, I am in no hurry to say what I must say. But Catherine, is yours so very bad?'

The concern in his dark eyes ripped at her heart. She nodded wordlessly, poured herself some tea and began. 'It was four years ago.' The cup in her hand shook. She put it carefully down on the table next to her.

'Wait.' Nicholas stirred the fire up brighter, then brought his glass across to sit next to her on the sofa. 'Drink your tea,' he said. 'We have all evening and there is no sense letting it go cold. Do you wish for your shawl?'

Not if you are next to me keeping off the demons. 'No, you have made it beautifully warm in here, thank you.' She drank a mouthful of tea, let the comfort of it seep into her and fixed her eyes on the flames. 'As I said, it was four years ago. Ann was asleep, I was mending one of Simon's shirts and he was home for once. He seemed on edge, but that was nothing strange. I was newly expecting and feeling ill, so when there was a knock on the door I was glad, because if it was Simon's card-playing friends, I could take the mending into the bedroom and doze over it instead of having to make conversation. Simon answered the door. I had already gathered up the shirt and turned to go when my arms were grabbed from behind and a hood dropped over my head. 'Orders' said a rough voice. 'You know who from.' Then I was taken outside, pushed into a carriage and taken away.'

Beside her, Nicholas jerked upright. 'Your husband made no move to stop this?' he said incredulously. 'He didn't fight the man or protect you in any way?'

Kitty looked at him bleakly. 'He gave me my cloak.'

Nicholas took a hasty swig of wine. 'Go on,' he said, his voice grim. 'Where did they take you?'

Kitty sipped some more tea, then set the cup down, not trusting herself not to drop it. This was even more difficult than she'd thought it would be. 'I do not know where we went, I couldn't see anything. My sense is that the journey was not a long one. I know because the man twisted my arms together behind my back and fondled me. There was not time for anything else.'

Next to her, Nicholas swore and put his arm around her. She took a shallow breath and continued, everything flooding back, just as if it had been half an hour ago, not four years. She could almost feel the hood over her face.

'I was pushed up narrow, echoing wooden stairs and into a room that didn't echo, but didn't feel richly furnished. I heard the man leave. I heard the bolt drawn on the outside of the door. I was quite alone. Then I heard another door open at the far end of the room and the sound of movement. Quiet footsteps this time, two sets. I didn't dare move. I was terrified. One of the men told me in a cold whisper to strip, but to leave the hood on. Everything he said was in cold whispers. It was all impersonal. Entirely remote. *Walk forward, stop, turn left, walk forward, raise your arms, bend.'*

'Catherine . . . ' Now both Nicholas's arms were around her, holding her to him, warming the icy shudders that the knife-sharp memories brought with them. She burrowed into his chest.

'There was a table in front of me. They tied my wrists and ankles to it. I thought I knew what was coming, but I was wrong. They whipped me, Nicholas, standing one each side, across my back, my buttocks, my legs. They did it deliberately, and with enjoyment. Not fast, but placing each stroke. Over and over. I thought they would never stop.'

She was shaking now, remembering. He held her closer and she could feel the weals on her back as another blow landed, and another . . .

'I will kill them,' he said hoarsely. 'So help me God, I will find them and I will kill them and I will burn their filthy house to the ground.'

'I passed out several times, and took

care to remain still whenever I came round. It was pure animal instinct by then. I don't know how long it was before they threw the cloak at me, bundled my dress and stays in my arms, banged on the door for it to be unbolted and withdrew on light, quick feet. The same rough man took me home. He did have his way with me this time. I screamed so hard I am amazed the horse didn't bolt. I was pushed out of the carriage on to my doorstep. I don't know how I climbed the stairs. I stumbled inside and told Simon to get Molly, then I fell on the bed and couldn't move until she'd washed off the blood and patched me up. I lost the child. It didn't survive the abuse. When I came to myself, I found a dressed flint in the pocket of my cloak. I couldn't think how it had got there. I put it out of Ann's way and didn't notice when it disappeared. It wasn't until this week — after we had been to Kennet End — that I realised it was his sign. His receipt.'

Nicholas still held her. His voice was thick with hatred. 'Your husband used you as a whipping boy to pay a debt to Flint.'

'That is what I believed. It killed any lingering feelings I had for him stone dead. And he *had* been cheating Flint. He said so later. He had thought himself favoured. His error. But I think my whipping was also a threat. Flint was saying that if Simon disobeyed him again, he would mete out a similar punishment to *him*. I told you Simon was afraid of physical violence. Seeing what they'd done to me — having the evidence before him every time he looked at my back — would have kept him subservient for years.'

'There are not words enough to convey my hatred and contempt and bile,' said Nicholas. 'Your husband deserved to die, and that it happened by Flint's hand is only justice. I think you are right — you were to be a permanent example. I have seen the bodies of women, whipped and worse

285

in the same way that you describe, where the perpetrator did not desist. Until now, we did not know those poor creatures were also part of Flint's catalogue of crimes. You have supplied us with an important link, though it chokes me to the soul that it was you. He must be stopped.'

Kitty took another breath and eased herself away from his chest so she could meet his eyes. 'This is where my last piece of information might help. It is also why I must always be in danger from him, regardless of what he thinks Simon might have told me. The whole time I was in that terrible room, I had the very strong impression that I did not count as a person. I could have been anyone, any female. They did not speak, they did not even tell my *why* they were beating me. My feeling was that to those two silent men, I did not really exist. I was an example, yes, but I was also a vessel for their utter scorn and hatred of all females. Whipping me excited them. Their breathing grew faster. I could smell their enjoyment. I could see nothing because of the hood, I could feel nothing but pain, but I am familiar with the sounds men make during sex. They would stop the whipping from time to time and then start again. Before I fainted the last time, I am certain they were taking each other.'

Nicholas sat bolt upright, locking eyes with her. 'Flint prefers men to women? Are you sure, Catherine?'

She nodded. 'I am sure.'

'I must let the others know. If this is true, it is tremendously important. Why did you not say anything before?'

'Because before this week I did not know beyond all doubt that one of the men in that room *was* Flint. You must know that in general he employs toughs to administer his beatings. Anyone would assume it was them who whipped me, not Flint himself. Because of the way it happened, and the silence, I had suspicions but no proof. One cannot identify whispers. I didn't *know*, Nicholas. Not until Billy mentioned the *two quiet gentlemen* who searched my rooms and I remembered the two silent men in that place. Not until we found the nodule of flint hidden in my father's desk and I recollected the one that had been in my cloak. And the very fact of it seemed so fantastic. Flint is a byword for fear on the streets, but nobody has *ever* mentioned his sexual proclivities; not a whisper, not a suspicion of a rumour. How could I even begin to think of it? Even Simon was unaware, I think. In our shifting, precarious community, that is extraordinary. He has been very, very careful.'

'With good reason,' said Nicholas. 'He can hide murder and extortion behind his shadowy persona, but preferring men is a crime directly attributable to himself.'

'Exactly so. If I said anything at all about that, it would get back to him and then I would be dead for sure. Indeed, now I know it was him, I believe it is only due to my fainting so comprehensively at the time that I am still alive.'

Nicholas's voice was low. 'And you have entrusted me with this knowledge. I don't know when I have ever been so honoured, or felt so humbled.' His eyes were deep pools of honesty as he gazed steadily at her. 'You trust me to keep you safe?'

Kitty swallowed, unable to look away. 'I trust you to get Ann to Rooke Hall if it becomes necessary. I do not care overmuch about myself.'

'It is as well I do then.'

He cared about her? He still cared? 'Even though I have been used by many men?' she choked out. 'Even though you now know I am scarred?'

He cupped her face. 'What difference does that make? I have felt no scars these past three nights, but even if I had, it would not be a reason to turn away.'

'As to that, Molly is talented with vinegar water and honey. It is another reason why I must do my best to ensure she is comfortable here and that her laundry prospers. But Nicholas, if you are not repulsed then I do not understand why you . . . '

'There were no more repeats?'

Kitty shook her head. 'That is not Flint's way. One crime, one punishment. Wiped out. And it worked. Simon didn't try to cheat Flint again until this year. He got blasé about the danger, I think, and was deep in debt. He and the woman who managed one of the accommodation houses formed a scheme to keep some of the profits before they were declared to Flint. That was the house in Hart Street that Flint burned down. Once that happened, Simon knew his pain-free days were numbered. It was what made him desperate enough to kidnap Verity. I am only glad he did not think to sell Ann. I don't believe even the fact that she was his own daughter would have stopped him.'

She found herself crushed so hard to Nicholas that she could barely breathe.

'I have said it before,' he growled. 'I

will no doubt go on saying it until the end of time. I wish he were not dead so I could have the satisfaction of thrashing him myself. Always providing I could let go of you to do it, which at the moment seems beyond my capability.'

A tentative warmth tried to take hold of Kitty. 'Nicholas, I do not understand. If this is pity, I will take it gladly, but earlier this evening, you said . . . '

To her surprise, he buried his head in her shoulder. 'I do not know why you listen to all the foolish things I say. No one else pays them any heed. Catherine, if you think for one moment that I would let you be by yourself tonight, you have made a very poor reading of my character.'

He was not rejecting her? He didn't find her abhorrent?

'Then . . . shall we retire?' she asked, still not quite believing it.

His kiss left her in no doubt. 'You see to the hot water. I'll see to the fire.'

12

They slept late the next morning. When Kitty stirred, Nicholas was still there, solid and protective at her back.

'Do you mind?' he asked, nuzzling into her neck. 'Will it discompose you if Ann finds me here? Say the word and I will go to my own room.'

She turned in his arms, still incredulous at her good fortune, feeling warmly, deliciously safe. 'I like you being here. I will tell Ann when I wake her that you are sharing my bed from time to time.'

There was a tiny stillness at that, but all he said was, 'You do not need to wake her just yet.'

'Nicholas, I must rise. Kitchens do not prepare themselves in the mornings.'

'Rising was what I had in mind too,' he murmured, kissing her slowly and lingeringly, with the result that she was even later going downstairs.

'Hot water's all ready for you, mum,' said Mrs Green, 'and Mrs Turner said to tell you they'd be sorting themselves out now all her goods have arrived.'

'Thank you,' said Kitty, striving for a collected air. She smiled at Mrs Green's niece. 'What a good job you have made of the floor this morning, Eliza. I daresay Ann and I could eat our breakfasts off it, it is so clean.'

Eliza's round face turned pink with pleasure. Mrs Green was no less diverted and Kitty escaped thankfully back upstairs with the water. She still did not understand Nicholas's change of heart, but for the sake of her domestic arrangements, it was probably just as well he would be returning to London next week.

★ ★ ★

Nick lay propped up with his hands behind his head watching Catherine

293

wash. He was enormously humbled and pleased that she trusted him enough not to banish him during her toilette. The mass of thin white lines covering her back filled him with anger, but he was well versed in channelling rage into a place in his mind where he could call on it at need.

'You are beautiful,' he said. 'Having met your brother, I must assume your mother was a lovely woman.'

Catherine turned with a smile, deftly keeping out of arm's reach as she slipped on her chemise and started to lace her stays. 'She was. And all my father wanted her for was the fifteen thousand pounds.'

I would take you with nothing at all. Nick sat up abruptly, reaching for his robe. She had told him so many things that had required bravery and trust. Tonight he was going to have to do the same. And then . . . and then she would be within her rights to hate him. 'I had best shave and turn myself into the semblance of a gentleman, ready for the heath.' He kissed her, unable to deny himself the touch of her lips for what might prove to be the last time. 'I will vacate the field for your daughter.'

★   ★   ★

'Mama . . . ?'

Kitty roused from her reverie to find Ann looking at her hopefully over the rim of her bowl of oatmeal. 'Yes?'

'Mama, if Mr Grimes is here for always now, does that mean we can ride in his hackney carriage?'

'I daresay we could, if he is not taking anyone else somewhere. But we scarce need to. Newmarket is not so big that we cannot walk from one end to the other.'

Ann gave an excited wriggle. 'We could visit Lottie. She said she has fields and fields to run in. And her mama asked us.'

Kitty stared at her daughter. *Out of the mouths of babes . . .* 'We could,' she said, then added casually, 'Jenny also asked if you might like to stay overnight at Rooke Hall with Lottie sometimes? Some of Papa's bad friends are looking for us. Mr Dacre says he will catch them, but I think he will need help. If I know you are safe with Adam and Jenny, I will be able to help him properly. Would that be all right?'

Ann nodded mutely, her eyes wide and apprehensive. 'Will he catch them all?' she asked.

'He is going to have a damn good try,' replied Nicholas, coming through the door. 'Good morning, Ann.'

'Good morning. With your sword?' asked Ann.

'With whatever I have to hand.'

Kitty blinked. 'What do you know of Mr Dacre's sword, pray?'

'He is going to teach me to fight with it so I can kill all the bad men.' Ann brandished her spoon above her head, stabbing unseen foes.

'Goodness, I appear to have bred an Amazon.'

Ann giggled.

'It will do her no harm to learn, if you have no objection,' said Nicholas. 'I started fencing when I was her age. I still have the practice foil I was taught with. I will bring it back from London with me when I return.'

He was intending to come back then. Kitty ducked her head, joy flooding her, then laughed aloud at Nicholas's expression as he took in the oatmeal porridge Ann was eating. 'Don't worry, I have bacon and a bowl of eggs for you,' she said in reassurance.

'Tonight we are having rabbit,' chattered Ann. 'Mama made a sling yesterday and killed one. Dicky was *dazzled.*'

Nicholas laughed. 'You remembered the way of it then? May I see?'

Kitty passed the braided sling across. 'Yes, but I must rework the end knot. It is not heavy enough to give enough speed to the pebble. Yesterday's rabbit was pure luck, though we are not telling Molly's son that.' She took it back and put it absently in her pocket. 'Oh, I still

297

have your ring in my reticule. I will give it to you before you go out.'

'Thank you. I missed it on my finger yesterday.'

Kitty gave him a quick smile as she started to fry bacon and crack eggs into a bowl. 'I thought that when I put on my mother's pearl ring. It is strange, the things that become part of your life without you ever noticing.'

A shadow passed across his face, but all he said was, 'Once I've eaten I will fetch Satan's spare tack from the livery stables and see if Thomson has returned with the greys, though when I'm to take them to Cheveley is a puzzle. It will be a busy day on the course today. There are two handicap sweepstakes as well as the Audley End stakes.'

Kitty attempted to look intelligent, but suspected from his chuckle that she'd failed utterly.

While he finished eating, she slipped outside to intercept Molly coming down the drive.

'And where were you this morning?' her friend asked with a sly wink.

Kitty flushed. 'You know very well, though I thought from what Nicholas said yesterday that I would not be. That man is more confusing than a street juggler. I told him about being used to pay Simon's debts *and* the whipping. He . . . doesn't hate me for it.'

'And why should he? I did a good job on your back, even if I do say so myself. You can't beat vinegar water for wounds and a crock of honey slathered on top.'

'And your lovely self sending Simon out to earn the money to pay for it, though I shudder to think of the fate of whoever he fleeced. I shall be forever grateful.'

'Hush, you'd do the same for me. Here, I got you a loaf as I guessed you were still dancing the featherbed jig. That's a penny you owe me. To tell the truth, I was late myself. The gentlemen are all out bothering anyone in a skirt already.' To Kitty's astonishment, she coloured. 'Fred was waiting up when I got back and I had to thank him for looking after Dicky on the journey, didn't I? He's a good man. Clear sighted, which a lot of 'em aren't.'

Whilst Kitty was still assimilating this, her friend's expression changed again. She turned, hands on hips, looking up the drive. 'Well, of all the prize gudgeons,' she said. 'He must have followed me back last night to see where I lived. What does he think he's doing here at this hour? It's not laundry he's after, that's for sure. Don't fret, he's harmless. I'll send him on his way.'

Kitty followed her gaze, curious to see which importunate client had become so inconveniently enamoured that he had followed Molly home.

A gentleman hesitated at the head of the drive, evidently taken aback at seeing two women gossiping together. Then the sunlight fell on his face and Kitty's heart thumped. Were her eyes deceiving her? It was John! Her brother John was moving forward, walking towards them. Lord above, was *John* the gentleman Molly had told her about? The one who had been looking for company because his wife was increasing and neglecting him?

'I'll go,' she said, and started up the drive, but just as she was wondering how to tell one's estranged brother that he shouldn't be visiting his light o' love in broad daylight on his sister's property, an ostentatiously smart carriage clattered to a halt behind him and an elegant but most definitely increasing lady alighted.

'Mr Bowman!' the vision cried out in accents signalling the end of the world.

John stopped dead, his face appalled.

'Mr Bowman, what are you doing here?' came the voice of doom again.

John's mouth opened weakly but no sound emerged.

And because he was merely stupid and pompous, not vicious, and he was her brother and they used to be friends, Kitty smoothed down her apron and advanced past John towards the virago with a welcoming smile on her face and her hand outstretched. She did not think she had ever seen such a look of complete astonishment on her brother's face as she passed him in all the years she'd known him.

'Good morning, you must be Mrs Bowman. John and Verity said you were very beautiful, and I see they were telling nothing but the truth. I am so pleased to meet you. I am Catherine Redding, John's sister. He has not mentioned me to you because I left home in disgrace and he did not want the slightest breath of scandal to touch you. However, since then I have been married and widowed again, and am now back in Newmarket to act as Verity's housekeeper. I wished very much to call on you, but did not quite dare.'

Her hand was shaken, but distractedly. 'I . . . Mrs Redding? That was not the name I heard . . . '

Kitty put on a brave look. 'Alas, I married Captain Eastwick in all faith before I discovered my mistake and we parted. My second husband was a good, kind man, but sadly suffered from ill health which is why you find me returned to the town of my birth after all these years.'

The virago wavered. 'John?' she said uncertainly.

Kitty's brother hurried to his wife's side and took her arm. 'Selena dearest, whatever possessed you to come out this early in the day? And when there is a race meeting taking place too. I am persuaded you should still be resting. Where is your mother? I am sure she would say the same. If I had known you wished to shop, I would have accompanied you both to Bury St Edmunds. My dear, it is as my sister says: I wished to spare you and your excellent mother any scandal, but as it appears all is now happily revealed, will you allow me to present my sister Catherine to you?'

'I am pleased to make your acquaintance,' said Selena faintly.

'Do please step inside,' said Kitty,

wondering how she was going to explain away the lack of any sort of maid. 'I am afraid all is in considerable disarray, for I only arrived this week and am readying the house for when Verity and Mr Congreve come here after their wedding. Indeed, I was just stepping down to my friend Mrs Turner to ask if she might assist me with shaking out curtains. Mrs Turner and her mother accompanied me here from London. They are opening a laundry at the back of the house. I daresay your own laundry maids see to all the Kennet End linen, but Mrs Turner is also a very fine seamstress if you ever have anything in need of mending. I am sure she would be most grateful for any recommendation you might be able to make to your friends.'

'I . . . Yes, I . . . '

'My dear, you are overwrought,' said John in solicitous tones. 'I see now I was wrong and should have disclosed Catherine's presence the moment I knew of it, so as to let you become accustomed to the idea gradually. As you can see, this is a perfectly respectable house, if a trifle eccentric; but what else would we both expect from Verity? I could wish her marriage would steady her — I told you I have heard good reports of Mr Congreve — but it seems sadly unlikely. Let me accompany you home now before I go up to the heath, and perhaps we might invite Catherine to call on us at Kennet End when you are feeling more the thing.'

'Indeed, I should very much like to visit one day to show my daughter the house of my childhood,' Kitty assured them earnestly. 'I daresay you will have made a great many elegant changes. I can see by your carriage and your costume that you have a most superior style.'

'I flatter myself that I do. Yes, perhaps that would be best. I do feel a little faint.'

'Then you must return home straight away,' said John, 'and I will fetch my horse from the livery stable and follow to see you safely back. It will not matter in the least if I delay meeting my friends.' He turned to Kitty. 'I am afraid we must put off our talk, sister.'

'Certainly, brother. It is of no moment at all. Send a note when it is convenient for me and Ann to call. Mrs Redding at Furze House will always find me.'

She saw his lips repeat *Mrs Redding* soundlessly as if committing it to memory, then she waved her newly-discovered sister-in-law off before collapsing on Molly's shoulder with helpless laughter.

'Well, who'd have thought he'd have the gumption to follow me,' marvelled Molly. Then her voice changed. 'And there's another. The guvnor's going to have to order us a set of fancy gates if it goes on like this. Oh Lord! Kitty quick, get inside before he sees you!'

Kitty looked towards the road. And fled into the house. She hadn't known his name, but she knew the face. She also knew the green ribbons threaded into his boots. 'Dear God, they have found me,' she whispered, pressing her back against the door. She had to get Ann to Rooke Hall. Fast.

★ ★ ★

Nick opened the front door as the garish coach made a stately turn between the gateposts and headed back down the High Street. He pulled on his gloves, still chuckling. What a prime idiot Catherine's brother was. He was looking forward to hearing the full story from her after he'd collected his tack and paid his shot at the livery stables.

But in the act of pulling the door shut, he froze. Where the carriage had just been, Viscount Perivale was now standing. Nick saw his victorious look as he sighted Catherine. And then Perry leisurely turned his head to con the rest of the house and he saw Nick himself.

Nick was back inside and shooting the bolt without thinking twice.

Catherine pelted down the hallway,

white and shaking. 'Viscount Perivale,' she said, her teeth chattering. 'He saw me. He knows where I live. I must get Ann away to Rooke Hall. I must do it now. I won't have her a pawn in this. Oh, why did I not send her with Jenny Prettyman two days ago?'

Nick took her arms and held her fast, feeling her struggle to be free, to snatch up Ann and run with her. 'Hush my love. Think. We have time. Perry cannot hope to storm this house on his own. Nor can he follow us if we leave immediately.'

'Fred Grimes's hackney . . . '

'Too slow. Satan is in the stable. I can take you both up before me, we can get through the back gate and be on the Fordham Road before he is mounted. Satan will gallop faster than anything Perivale can hire from the inn.'

She nodded, gave a gasping sob and darted away, flying to get Ann into outdoor shoes and snatching up her reticule and a cloak to cover them both. Nick sprinted out of the side door towards the stable. Never had he valued more the ability to saddle a horse on his own without the benefit of grooms or ostlers.

13

'Rooke Hall is three or four miles towards Fordham,' said Catherine, raising her voice to make herself heard over Satan's thudding hooves. 'There is a wooded part along this road, then open fields and a lane off to the right between hedgerows. Hopefully there will be a board. I *think* I will know the turning when I see it, but it is a very long time since I was last here.'

Nick grunted to show he'd heard, concentrating on passing the plodding tradesmen's carts in both directions and avoiding the lively sporting curricles heading for Newmarket and the heath.

'In case I forget to mention it,' added Catherine, 'you are a quite superb rider.'

Warmth spread through his limbs. Even at moments like this, she contrived to bolster him. It was going to be very difficult to give her up.

She was murmuring to her daughter now. 'Are you all right? Not squashed?'

Nick risked a quick look down past Catherine's shoulder. Ann was peeping out of her mother's cloak, her eyes shining.

'It's *exciting*,' came her thrilled whisper.

Nick swallowed and redoubled his concentration. Pray God this would live in the little girl's memory as an adventure. Ann was the most important person in Catherine's world. It was up to him to keep both of them safe. Even as he thought it, the responsibility settled into his skin and became part of him. Let Perry do his worst. Nick was ready.

★ ★ ★

'You are returning with me to Furze House?' Nick injected astonishment into his voice in a bid to persuade Catherine to stay at Rooke Hall.

'You know I am,' she said. 'Ann is

311

safe here and I refuse to spend the rest of my life looking over my shoulder.' She kissed her daughter and turned to take her leave of Jenny.

'You don't wish me to accompany you?' said Adam to Nick in a low voice. 'Perivale does not know me.'

Nick hesitated. It was very tempting, but Catherine was depending on Adam to guard her daughter. It was why they were here. And he still had difficulty thinking of Perry as an out-and-out villain. Surely a promise of funds to settle his debts would be enough to have the man returning to London saying he hadn't been able to trace Captain Eastwick's wife.

He said as much to Adam. 'I will take Catherine back and then go hunting our friend. If it turns out I am mistaken and Perivale is more of a rogue than I've bargained for, well then, I am not so useful to the world that I will be a great loss. One way or another, he will not betray her whereabouts to Flint.'

'That is no attitude to take into a

fight,' said Adam. 'You had best find yourself a little anger, my friend.'

Nick grinned and buffeted him absently on the shoulder, but he stood by his statement. If this week had shown him anything it was that there was nothing for him in his grandfather's house. There was no reason to look forward to a return to London and his sham of a life. He cared for nothing sufficient to make any act of bravery seem foolhardy.

Catherine turned from her conversation with Jenny and smiled at him. 'I am ready,' she said.

Until now, he realised. *Oh my Lord. Until now.*

⋆ ⋆ ⋆

Nick strove to keep this new and astounding revelation to himself. He couldn't fathom how he had not already realised he was in love with her, but whatever the reason, no good could come from telling Catherine how he

313

felt. Instead, for the first twenty minutes of their rather more sensibly-paced ride home, they discussed ways by which they might decoy Viscount Perivale into a trap and persuade him to reveal Flint's identity. Both knew it had to take place before the man reached London.

'I could walk openly past the White Hart and lead him into a blind alley where you are concealed,' suggested Catherine.

'Concealed behind what? A pile of rotting rubbish? And all the other denizens of the alley conveniently absent? Not on any account. A gambling den would do it with Adam to play doorman, but Perivale won't believe me now if I tell him there's a new one opened. Possibly if Alex Rothwell mentions one within earshot . . . '

'Would he not make up a party with his friends to try it out? Oh, what if I advertised a card party in Furze House? We could use that terrifying morning room. Hire some tables for it from the furniture broker and return them quickly, before the woodworm moves in.'

Nick tightened his grip on her waist. 'Tell me, have your schemes always come with a death wish? I believe my best plan is to ascertain his bedchamber at the White Hart and bribe the chambermaid to let me in.'

Catherine sighed. 'Unexciting, but more likely to succeed. It is a shame he had no money on him a couple of nights back. Molly would already know the room if he had been in funds. We could ask her anyway.'

'The Furze House Irregulars living up to their name, eh?'

She chuckled. 'Why not? We do have sources of information you have no access to. Oh, that gives me another idea . . . '

Two miles from Newmarket, trotting through a long wooded stretch that bore gently to the right, Nick was repeating forcefully that he wasn't having either her or Molly setting themselves up as lures to draw the man in, when their progress was abruptly halted by the crack of a pistol and a bullet whistling past Nick's cheek so closely he felt its path. Satan bucked and plunged down the wooded bank to the left. Nick caught just a glimpse of a greatcoated figure between the trees before they were in amongst them, Satan trampling mast and dead branches to find a foothold.

'Footpads,' said Nick in disbelief. 'In broad daylight, damn them.'

'A footpad with green ribbons,' replied Catherine thinly. 'Just the one.'

Nick swore. 'Then we'll outrun him. Sit as low as you can.' He bent forward, pressing on Satan's flank to guide him towards a break in the trees. 'On boy, fast as you like.'

There was another shot. Satan veered sharply and to his horror, Nick felt Catherine slip sideways from his grasp and fall to the ground. He regained control of the spooked horse and wheeled around but he was too late. Viscount Perivale was running towards Catherine, pistol cocked and ready to fire.

'Leave, Dacre,' said Perry in an ugly voice. 'I've no quarrel with you. It's Mrs Eastwick I want.'

'The devil I will.' Nick considered riding at the man and knocking him down, but the ground was strewn with tree roots and fallen branches. Satan would have a broken leg and he'd be dead from Perry's gun before he'd got six yards. Instead he swung down from the saddle and closed the gap between them, fists clenched, murder in his heart.

Perry swivelled around and trained his pistol on Nick's chest. 'You fool, you could have carried on riding. You'd have been free and clear in two minutes,' he said. 'No doxy is worth this. Do you *want* me to kill you?'

A surge of irrational anger filled Nick at the sight of the green ribbons flapping on Perivale's boots. A woman's life and liberty at stake — yet Perry was still continuing to make himself look ridiculous for the sake of a bet.

'How did you find us?' asked

Catherine. She'd let the hood of her cloak fall back, loosened her neckline and had her gaze fixed on Perry with what Nick would have sworn was admiration if he hadn't known better. As she spoke, she sank to a fallen tree and rubbed her ankle as if she'd twisted it in falling. Nick's blind rage fell away, reason reasserted itself. *Oh, you clever woman. Pile on the flattery. Keep him talking so I can rush him.*

Astoundingly, it worked. Viscount Perivale's chest expanded. 'Ha! Devilish recognisable, Dacre, that's your problem. I've told you so before. All I had to do was ask about that black charger of yours and no end of people told me how they'd seen you riding hell for leather along the road to Fordham. Of course, I knew that had to be a blind to persuade me you'd gone that way. It didn't fool me though. I made sure you'd be doubling back and heading out on the other road, the one to Mrs Eastwick's brother's place. And here you are doubling back, just as I said.'

'Clever,' murmured Nick.

'I was right about Bowman too, wasn't I? Not receiving visitors indeed. What a hum. I knew if I kept following him I'd find his sister. Well, you've led me a fine dance, little lady, but the game's up.' He ogled her neckline lasciviously, already anticipating success. 'I'll make you an offer, my dear. You play with me nicely and I won't shoot your Sir Galahad here. Can't say fairer than that. I won't even tell my employer about him. How's that for generous?'

Catherine sighed and reached for her reticule as if she was giving in. It had fallen to the ground when she'd slipped and now lay a little way away.

Nick couldn't believe she'd bought Perivale's line. She must have something in mind. It was imperative he kept him talking. 'This man you do commissions for, Perry,' he said, moving slightly to the side to increase the gap between himself and Catherine. 'Do you know what he does?'

Perry smiled widely, realigning the

pistol. 'Why yes. He kills people who don't deliver.'

'He tortures innocents. He inflicts pain for no other reason than that he enjoys it. What did he tell you to do, Perry?'

'To find Mrs Eastwick. He said she'd roll up here. He said she used to be Miss Bowman of Kennet End, and blood always wins. He said family is where you go when the chips run out. He was right, wasn't he?'

'Why did he want her?'

'No idea. Didn't ask. Not my business.'

'And what were you to do with her?'

'Anything I liked. Game little piece. Married to Eastwick she'd have to be, wouldn't she? She's not the innocent she makes out, you know. All sorts of stories about her if you listen to the gossip at the tables. I was looking forward to amusing myself with her. Still am.'

'Uniformly charming as always, Perry. Then what? Let her go?'

Perivale gave him a reproachful look. 'Come, Dacre, you know better than that. He wanted her dead or delivered. He didn't say in what condition.'

Nick's voice grew remote. 'And you were happy with that, were you?'

Perivale shrugged. 'Why shouldn't I be? It was her or me.'

'You are completely loathsome.'

'That's easy for you to say. You don't owe as much as I do. And you've got family to back you up. They'll never let your name get dragged through the mud.'

'So have you got a good name. You've never thought of taking the honourable way out of your difficulties?'

Mock reflection filled Perivale's face. 'No,' he said, shaking his head.

'Then I must do it for you.'

His adversary gave a shout of genuine laughter. 'I'd like to see you try when I'm the one with the gun.'

Nick made a careless gesture, easing another step away from Catherine. 'I still have my fists. I'm curious, Perry.

321

You're independent. Good family. How did you get into our friend's coils?'

'How does anyone? Money, dear boy. The Black & White Club on Piccadilly. Do you know it?'

'Where everyone must wear black or white. I went there once. I can't say it appealed to me.'

'Oh, I don't know. The play is decent.'

'The play is always decent at first, Perry. Then you start losing.'

'I'd have come about. Thing is, *before* I came about, I was offered a sweet little deal. Collect a wad of the folding stuff from that opium den on Wardour Street and spend it all at the E-O table in the Black & White. What I won, I could keep. But I had to spend it all first, see?'

The Black & White Club. Long rumoured to be one of Flint's enterprises. So that's how the money was processed between his outlets. 'I fail to see the difficulty. Betting on the tables has never been a problem with you.'

'Not in the ordinary way, no, but

there's this fellow who was becoming dashed unpleasant, so I took to slipping him a bit en route.'

Nick made pained face. 'Far be it from me to criticise, but it seems a little optimistic to assume your employer wouldn't know how much you had collected.'

'Devil and the deep blue sea, Dacre. Both of them break legs. I was going to put my winnings on the E-O wheel to make up for it, but there didn't always seem to be quite enough. It was getting to be rather a close-run thing. Then on Saturday I was offered this job. Turns out Flint knew about my fellow all the time. Mrs Eastwick was to cancel out the debt and I'd still keep the E-O arrangement. All would be well.'

'Suppose you didn't find her?'

'Use your head, man. I'd still have the debt, wouldn't I? Besides, I *have* found her.'

'He doesn't know that. Not unless you've sent him a note.'

'What, and have someone else poach her before I can get her to him? Not likely. Besides, where would I send it? Care of Flint, The George, London? I don't think so.'

The George. One of the large sprawling inns near Drury Lane. And interestingly, the one where Molly Turner didn't want to be taken for supper that time. He would have to have another word with her about that. 'Is that where you are to take her?'

'What's it matter to you? Give up on her, Dacre. Find yourself another. Plenty more lightskirts where she came from. Ones with more meat on them.'

All this time, Nick had seen out of the corner of his eye, Catherine sitting dejectedly on the fallen tree, seemingly resigned to her fate. He had seen her fiddling with a golden cord that had apparently become detached from her reticule. He had seen her despondently picking up small pebbles from the ground. *Clever, clever girl.* He took another small step away, keeping Perivale's attention on him. All he needed was a tiny distraction from

Catherine, then he could rush the man and hit him with a punishing right, strong enough to break his jaw.

'It's not going to happen, Perry. She's under my protection.'

'Dashed inconvenient,' grumbled Viscount Perivale. 'Dammit, Dacre, I *like* you. Oh well . . . ' He sighted casually along the barrel of his pistol and pulled the trigger.

14

Concealed by her cloak, Kitty's fingers had been working fast, teasing the sling out of her pocket, feeling on the ground for stones of the right size. One hit was all the distraction she needed. Then she could launch herself at Viscount Perivale and hang on to his arm for long enough to stop him shooting Nicholas.

She'd looped the eye of the sling over her middle finger before she remembered the knot at the end. It wasn't sufficiently weighted! At this range, she needed something heavy there or the projectile wouldn't fly true. Could she work a stone into it? Was there time? Or . . . her frantic gaze fell on her reticule. Oh, oh yes . . . Feeling inside very carefully, her heart thumped in relief as Nicholas's ring — his lovely, heavy, bloodstone ring — slipped on to her finger. Withdrawing it quietly, she secured it to the end knot.

Nicholas was moving away, keeping Perivale turning so his profile was presented to her. That was helpful but the foolish man was taunting him at the same time. Did Nicholas not realise his own danger?

'It's not going to happen, Perry. She's under my protection.'

Terror ran through Kitty as Perivale's expression hardened and he sighted directly at Nicholas. *No!* In the instant before he pulled the trigger, Kitty swung back her arm and let the stone fly. It was a perfect shot to the temple and would have distracted him wonderfully . . .

. . . had it not been a devastating, heart-breaking quarter of a second too late.

Time slowed as the stone flew. Perivale's hand jerked as he squeezed the trigger. The sound ricocheted shockingly around the trees. Rooks erupted in a ragged cloud at the disturbance.

Nicholas fell forward.

'Nicholas,' screamed Kitty. She hurled

herself at Viscount Perivale, twisting his hands behind his back with strength she hadn't realised she possessed and tying them with her cord. 'Nicholas, say something. Don't be dead. Please don't be dead. I love you.' There was a roaring in her ears and a far away clapping of birds' wings, but nothing else. Kitty beat back a wail of anguish. 'Say something, Nicholas!'

'I'm not dead,' croaked Nicholas. He crawled towards her across the beech mast and broken branches, a hand pressed awkwardly to his shoulder. 'Sweetheart, you are the most wonderful woman in the world and I love you. I don't suppose you've got a clean handkerchief in that reticule?'

He wasn't dead. He wasn't dead, but there was blood seeping between his fingers. A lot of blood. Nervelessly, Kitty let Perivale fall to the ground and pulled off her fichu, bundling it into a pad and cramming it inside Nicholas's coat.

'I need to bandage it,' she said frantically. 'I need to get this under your shirt and button your waistcoat and coat over the top. I'm sorry, Nicholas, I was too late to stop him. I shouldn't have wasted time tying on the ring.'

She was babbling. She took a sobbing breath to make herself stop. Only then did she realise Nicholas wasn't listening to her. He was gazing over her shoulder at Viscount Perivale. Viscount Perivale, who was oddly silent. She turned to look. Her hand went to her mouth.

'I don't think you needed to secure him,' said Nicholas in a strained voice. 'My God, it must have been a shot in a thousand. Untie his hands as fast as you can and put the sling back in your pocket. Quicldy, Catherine. Someone may have heard the shot and be coming to investigate. It will be a lot better for both of us if we aren't here.'

Kitty untied the cord, her fingers fumbling now, when they had been so sure before. 'What do you mean? What are we going to do? Nicholas, you need a doctor. You can't hide a bullet wound.'

'Flesh wound. I'm only winged, thanks to you. You disrupted his aim. But look, there is not a mark on Perry save the graze on his temple and that could be put down to his falling from his horse. If that isn't divine luck, I don't know what is. Where did he leave his mount? Ah, it's over there. I'll unhitch it from the tree and then we must both of us be actively elsewhere as soon as possible. The horse will be found by a passer-by. It won't take long on this road. Catherine . . . Catherine, my love, we must move fast. Have you left anything on the ground? No? Go and wait with Satan. You are going to have to help me steer him home, then bind my shoulder tight enough for me to get to the heath. Move, sweetheart. I love you more than life itself, but there is no need for either of us to hang if we don't have to.'

Kitty was still staring at their late adversary, shocked to her core. 'He was going to kill you,' she whispered. 'I had to stop him.'

'Yes, he was. I would have done the same, but you were quicker. For the love of God, get up and help me stand. If you have saved me only to let me bleed to death in a nameless wood, I shall not be impressed. We need to get home.'

She glanced irresolutely back the way they'd come. 'Not to Adam? It's faster.'

'Home. We have a story to give flesh to.' He gritted his teeth as she helped him up. 'Though I might ask Rothwell to send word to Caro to visit Jenny as soon as may be. If the horse is found while the racing fraternity are still in Newmarket, Perivale's unlucky fall will be established fact by the time everyone is back in London. It all aids the tale.'

Kitty assisted Nicholas in guiding Satan home, but it was sheer instinct. She was still in a daze. Viscount Perivale was dead. Flint wouldn't find her. Not yet. Not this time.

'Bernier's Wood,' she said, coming to herself as they approached the back gate of Furze House.

He roused. 'I beg your pardon?'

'Where Viscount Perivale ambushed us. It isn't nameless. It is called Bernier's Wood.'

'Oh . . . good.' He dismounted, catching at her arm for balance, then straightening up.

'I cannot believe you were ever a sickly, frail boy,' muttered Kitty. 'You have a constitution of iron. Fred, can you see to Satan, please? Molly, hurry, I need your help.'

★ ★ ★

Quite how Nick made it to the heath, he didn't know. He suspected the bumper of port-and-gin slipped to him by Ma Turner had something to do with it. His shoulder felt as if it was on fire, but the pad and bandage were secure and he managed to converse rationally with several groups of people before espying Alex Rothwell and heading over to him with considerable relief.

'Far be it from me to cast aspersions, Dacre, but your handling of the ribbons doesn't seem quite as polished as usual today.'

'Let us hope not everyone is as observant. In truth, I'm only staying in the saddle because Satan is such a gentleman,' replied Nick. 'Alex, can you get a message to your wife? Can she visit Jenny Prettyman this afternoon? If she could also possibly manage to find a stray horse and thus a dead man in what I am given to understand is called Bernier's Wood, I will be in her debt.'

His friend raised a well-bred eyebrow, but merely said, 'Certainly. Let me introduce you to my brother-in-law. He has any number of grooms at your disposal. Is it any particular dead man you would like Caro to find? I am afraid I must draw the line at her actually providing you with one.'

Nick gave an appreciative chuckle. 'Perivale. He intercepted us on the way back from Rooke Hall and winged me. The only reason you are not even now bearing bad news back to my grandfather is due entirely to Catherine's skill with a slingshot. She caught his temple just as he pulled the trigger. Stone dead.'

'Good Lord.'

'I have seen something similar before — a flush hit during a bare knuckle fight. There is an area of extreme fragility there. In general, as you know, a blow will leave the combatant unconscious. That once, I saw it kill.'

'Hence your very understandable need to be seen here on the course. Harry! Over here!' He beckoned to a pleasant red-haired man, held a quick conversation with him and returned. 'All in train. Shall we place our bets for the Audley End stakes now? How long can you hold up?'

'Long enough to run casually across Rutland, if you can steer us a path. I need to sort out a time to take the greys over to Cheveley. I hope he still wants them.'

'He would not back out now. Incidentally, we had best say you are engaged to dine with me tonight if anyone asks. I am inclined to accompany you back to Furze House as it is.'

'I would be very grateful, Alex.'

'And now I know you are unwell,' remarked his friend. 'How is Mrs Redding?'

'Shocked. Relieved. Bearing up. Completely wonderful. I did not like to leave her. I must get back to her as soon as I can.'

'Completely wonderful? Nick . . . ' There was concern in Alex's eyes.

'Yes. I know. You do not need to tell me.'

Because today I told her I loved her. And now I am going to break her heart.

* * *

'What do we do now? I do not make the mistake of thinking it is all over.'

It was evening, and the flames on the hearth were combining with the candle-light to create an illusion of a safe haven. Kitty knew it was a lie. She had

335

felt something building in Nicholas all evening. Was he afraid he had said too much earlier? She would not demur when he retracted it. She had heard him say he loved her. That truth would warm her for years.

Nicholas sighed. 'Tomorrow, my lord duke buys my greys. It is the last day of the Houghton meeting, which I must attend, and I will no doubt speculate along with everyone else about what can have befallen Viscount Perivale. Then the racing world will disperse to their various enjoyments and I . . . I shall stay here for a few days.'

'Here?' Kitty sat up in surprise. 'But I thought . . . '

'In London, I fill my days with riding, fencing and boxing, none of which I can do with an injured shoulder. Better to stay here if I may and give out that I am setting up my new venture.'

Why did he sound so wretched? Was he regretting it already? 'Set up your new venture with what?' she asked.

'Ah, there you have it. I will calculate

costs and returns and then go to see my grandfather. What I would then like to do is to come straight back here. But I am not sure I should.'

He was regretting it. Kitty fought to suppress the sharp pain in her breast. She had expected nothing more.

'I understand,' she said quietly.

'No, you don't. I tried to tell you yesterday, but your story was the more urgent as well as being rather more noble than mine. Catherine, I meant it when I said I loved you. This week I have not once drunk myself into a stupor, nor have I resorted to laudanum to help me sleep. I have had purpose for the first time in my life because of you. I do not know how I can do without you.'

Hope stole treacherous fingers around her heart. 'Then don't.'

'I must. You deserve someone who will protect you, someone who will give you a home and a family, someone who will surround you with security and spoil you with presents. You need someone safe like Adam, or caring like Charles. That is not going to happen if I am sharing your bed two weeks out of every four. No husband appreciates being cuckolded.'

He was thinking of staying with her that often? A smile broke out on her face. 'I do not want anyone else. Adam is large and safe and kind. Charles Congreve is a good man. But you, Nicholas, you stir my blood. You make me feel alive. You are part of me.'

'As you are me. There is more warmth in your smile than there is in all my grandfather's house. There is more arousal in one of your kisses than there has been passion in my whole life. You set me on fire with a touch, and soothe me with a look. But I can give you nothing honourable in return. No name, no money, no security.'

'I do not want anything.'

'This is madness, Catherine. Find a good man to love you, and, despite my appalling reputation, I will try very hard not to kill him.'

She cuddled next to him, pillowing her head on his good shoulder. 'You are feverish. There is not a good man in the country who would take on a woman twice involved in scandal, forced into prostitution to pay her husband's debts, beaten by the most feared man in London and who is still likely being hunted by him. I prefer you whenever you can get here, appalling reputation and all.'

He frowned. 'Twice? Twice involved in scandal?'

'Once when I eloped with Simon. And again when it is known that I am openly being kept by you. You have to admit, Nicholas, it makes a far better cover story for Furze House than the Pool setting up a respectable home for charitable boarders. That is what we will still say, of course, and no one will look into the unlikelihood of it, because Society, in its infinite wisdom, will know better. It is a beautiful scheme.'

'Damn, it really is.' There was reluctant admiration in his voice.

'Then that is settled.'

'Not quite. You are all that is beautiful and generous, but hear me out before you lay any more of your trust at my feet, for I do not deserve it. Catherine, I love you very much and with all my heart, but I cannot marry you.'

'No, of course you cannot,' she said. 'Nobody of quality could. I do not expect it. I told you that.'

'I would do it and damn the world if it were possible. But I can't. I am unable to marry you because . . . because I already have a wife.'

Kitty sat up in utter surprise. Nicholas was *married?* It was the one thing she had not expected. How could it be? He did not act married, he had never referred to a wife, and it went against everything she had thought of him that he would behave with such dishonour towards any woman he had made such a promise to.

He looked away from her. 'I knew you would be repulsed. I had no right to say anything to you of love. It was unforgivable. Please accept my apologies. I will behave with the utmost propriety from now on.'

There was just a moment when Kitty didn't know him at all. Then she studied his profile more closely. His eyes held the sheen of moisture, his lips were pressed rigidly together. She possessed herself of his hand. 'Tell me,' she said.

'Gentlemen don't explain,' he replied, addressing the corner of the room. 'They live with their actions. They take the consequences.'

'Is this more of your grandfather's code of conduct? Dacre rules? You are not him, Nicholas.'

Silence. Kitty waited.

A shudder went through him. 'No, I am not.' He turned his head and looked at her soberly. 'You are extremely good for me.' He took a fortifying breath. 'Power and position, that's what it comes down to. My grandfather, as I told you, thrives on having people dependent on him. The more children my uncles' wives produced, the better he liked it. When my cousins were of an age to marry and extend his dynasty, he was beside himself with power. My mother, on the other hand, grew less secure. Oh, she was the one in residence in the town house, she was the one who ran his public life, but she viewed all these potential pretenders for the throne as if they were enemy marauders camped outside the gates.'

'Yorkshire is hardly outside the gates of London,' said Kitty.

'Never underestimate a French emigre with paranoia,' replied Nicholas. 'She reasoned that she would be more secure if her one Dacre investment could have a child of his own. Unfortunately, I wasn't playing. I was young still. Learning, fencing, enjoying myself. I had seen my cousins' families, don't forget. I had no intention of tying myself down. I should have known better.'

He had relaxed while he was talking, but Kitty could feel the bitterness in his words. She leant against him.

'It did not occur to me, when my mother invited her own cousin's daughter to stay with her in London, that there was anything more in it than to introduce Silvie to English society. She made an instant hit, being very French, very lovely, and much more sophisticated than home-bred girls of the same age. My mother held a party for her; all the cousins were invited. They could see Silvie had my grandfather's favour — being just the sort of young woman to charm an elderly gentleman — and began competing for her. Competition amongst young men is fatally addictive. I'm not proud to say I strutted with the rest. They all hate me anyway as I am the one on the premises, the one my grandfather sees most often. It was heady stuff when Silvie appeared to prefer my company to that of my cousins. And when I found my least favourite cousin Donald taking liberties with her in the orangery and knocked him down, I thought myself no end of a fellow.'

Kitty saw what was coming now. He hadn't had a chance. 'Oh Nicholas.'

He gave her a twisted grin. 'Perspicacious, aren't you? Yes, you are quite right; Silvie was so, so grateful. Yes, she got me very drunk. Yes, she enticed me to her bedchamber. I almost ruined their plans, though, by waking in the dead of night, staggering back to my own room like a gentleman to comprehensively cast up my accounts, and then not emerging until the middle of the afternoon by which time any possibility of being discovered *in flagrante* was over. Thoroughly ashamed, I returned to Cambridge the next day and forgot about the incident. I assumed she would want to do the same. Come the vacation, I arrived home to be informed that Silvie was in an interesting condition, that she had confessed everything, and that I was expected to do the decent thing.'

'Which you did. Yes, I see. You could have done nothing else.'

'I could. I could have questioned the paternity. I could have pointed out that Silvie knew far more of what to do than I did. I could have evinced considerable surprise that I had, in fact, been in any condition to father a child at all that evening. But I was a Dacre, I had been brought up to be a gentleman at all times. I *had* made some sort of love to her, whoever had instigated it. I said nothing.'

'How long ago was this?'

'Eight years ago? Nine? The summer passed slowly. Silvie was ecstatic with her new apartment in the town house. She and my mother entered on an orgy of redecoration. I was not encouraged to enjoy the benefits of matrimony because she regretted infinitely, *mon cher*, that she felt altogether too fragile. I didn't care, being deep in self-disgust by then, though it did occur to me that her modiste was remarkably skilled in contriving that none of the signs of her pregnancy were visible. Then I was sent to Yorkshire on an errand about the estate. While I was there, Donald took delight in showing off the excellent points of a very fine stallion that had previously been in my grandfather's stable and that he had apparently been made a present of.'

'Subtle,' said Kitty drily.

'I returned home to the news that Silvie had suffered some sort of medical trauma and lost the baby. Her grief was as short-lived as it was theatrical. Within a fortnight she was back to shopping, dancing and flirting with every beau in town.'

'You disbelieved her?'

'Catherine, I am a Dacre. I disbelieved the whole pack of them. I discovered there had been no nurse engaged, no midwife and, crucially but typically of my family, the doctor had not been adequately recompensed for his sorry part in the deception and thus more than happy to talk to me. The entire thing had been planned. Silvie wanted wealth and position. My mother had wanted an ally in the house. My grandfather wanted me even more shackled and dependent on his good will than I was already. In this he was successful. The wedding had taken place in his presence, his own chaplain officiating and with his blessing. It could not be undone. Now do you see why I detest my family?'

'That is barbaric. To chain you for life like that!'

'My grandfather told me to stop fussing and be grateful they'd saved me the bother of finding a suitable bride for myself. He said Silvie was a pretty thing and knew the rules. I told him that as he had made the match, he could support her and enjoy the power of having someone else dependent on him. I then removed myself back to my bachelor rooms. Only once have I tried moving out of the house altogether. The curtailment of all funds, coinciding with a sudden lapse in health on my grandfather's part, brought me to heel again. You cannot conceive how much I hated myself for the weakness. Since then I have salved my conscience by righting wrongs in private wherever I could find them and making it my mission to be as scandalous in public as I possibly can.'

'Then the arrangement with me will

serve admirably,' said Kitty. 'I knew you would never behave with less than honour. Nicholas, I dare not return with you to London, but I will live with you here as your wife in all but name. I am yours, my love. There are no two ways about it. You have saved me so many times I could not separate myself from you if I tried.'

He met her gaze and she saw all the love she felt for him reflected back five-fold in his ardent, dark eyes.

'I am more honoured than I can say. I do not deserve such trust. Dearest Catherine, do you not know you have saved *me*? I have never even known simple affection until this week, let alone the sort of love I feel for you.' He bent his head and kissed her with a passion that said more adequately than any words just how he felt. Then he paused reflectively. 'If my grandfather sends someone with a banker's draft to buy you off whilst I am in London, take it. We are going to need to build a new stable on the land next door.'

'You will have to open me an account.'

'I will visit Hammond's bank first thing on Monday morning. Catherine, you truly don't mind that I am not legally free?'

'I truly don't. I love you. All I want is a small, safe life and you, whenever I can have you.'

'And Flint eradicated.'

'That too.'

'Then we will work on it. But for now, what do you say to just being Nicholas and Catherine, alone in the darkness?'

'You should rest your shoulder.'

'I have a very good nurse. She will ensure I do not overstrain myself. What do you say?'

She lifted her lips to his. 'Yes. I say yes. Now and forever, I say yes.'

Acknowledgements

Any mistakes are my own, but I owe
particular thanks to

Louise Allen, for not only being a fine
writer and the very best beta-reader and
sounding board for Regency ideas ever,
but also for writing 'Regency Slang
Revealed' and lending me her precious
'Domestic Cookery' book from 1807
https://www.louiseallenregency.co.uk/

Newmarket Local History Group for all
the work that has gone into collating
photos, plans and articles about Newmarket through the ages

Kate Johnson for endless support and
pointing out the bewildering bits

All my friends, both online and offline
for encouragement and nagging
and you, if I've forgotten to include you

We do hope that you have enjoyed reading this large print book.

Did you know that all of our titles are available for purchase?

We publish a wide range of high quality large print books including:
Romances, Mysteries, Classics
General Fiction
Non Fiction and Westerns

Special interest titles available in large print are:
The Little Oxford Dictionary
Music Book, Song Book
Hymn Book, Service Book

Also available from us courtesy of Oxford University Press:
Young Readers' Dictionary
(large print edition)
Young Readers' Thesaurus
(large print edition)

For further information or a free brochure, please contact us at:
Ulverscroft Large Print Books Ltd.,
The Green, Bradgate Road, Anstey,
Leicester, LE7 7FU, England.
Tel: (00 44) **0116 236 4325**
Fax: (00 44) **0116 234 0205**

GAY DEFEAT

Denise Robins

Disarmingly lovely, Delia Beringham is the only daughter of a wealthy financier who indulges her every whim. It is Delia's hope that her lover, Lionel Hewes, will leave his wife for her — but the sudden crash of the Beringham family fortune and her father's suicide change all that. Lionel abruptly fades from the picture, and Delia is left with only her own courage and determination to sustain her. So what is she to say when her father's friend, Martin Revell, chivalrously offers her his hand in marriage?

LORD SAWSBURY SEEKS A BRIDE

Fenella J. Miller

If he is to protect his estate and save his sister from penury, Lord Simon Sawsbury must marry an heiress. Annabel Burgoyne has no desire to marry, but wishes to please her parents, who are offering a magnificent dowry in the hope of enticing an impecunious aristocrat. As Simon and Bella, along with their families, move to their Grosvenor Square residences for the Season, it's not long before the neighbours are drawn together. But when events go from bad to worse, will Simon sacrifice his reputation to marry Bella?